MIXED

Tamar Hodes

This is a work of fiction. Names and characters are the product of the author's imagination and any resemblance to actual persons, living or dead, is entirely coincidental.

ISBN: 979-8-8051036-2-0

Also by Tamar Hodes

Raffy's Shapes

The Watercress Wife and Other Stories

One Hundred Short Escapes

The Water and the Wine

In memory of my father Aubrey Hodes (1927-2013)

who led me to reform Judaism and to writing

Contents

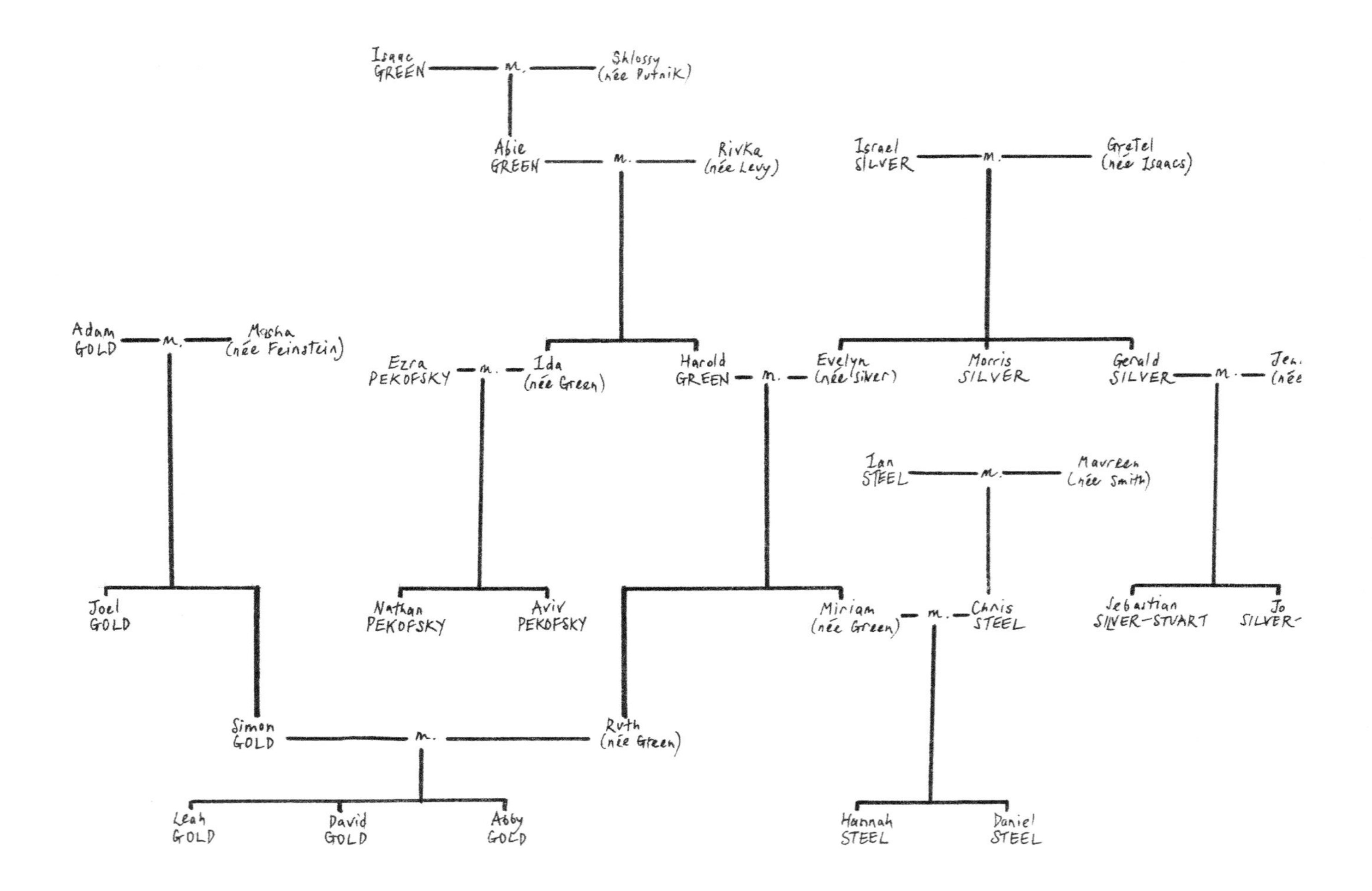

Isaac GREEN
m.
Shlossy (née Putnik)
Abie GREEN
m.
Rivka (née Levy)
Israel SILVER
m.
Gretel (née Isaacs)
Adam GOLD
m.
Masha (née Feinstein)
Ezra PEKOFSKY
m.
Ida (née Green)
Harold GREEN
m.
Evelyn (née Silver)
Morris SILVER
Gerald SILVER
m.
Jen (née
Ian STEEL
m.
Maureen (née Smith)
Joel GOLD
Nathan PEKOFSKY
Aviv PEKOFSKY
Miriam (née Green)
m.
Chris STEEL
Sebastian SILVER-STUART
Jo SILVER-
Simon GOLD
m.
Ruth (née Green)
Leah GOLD
David GOLD
Abby GOLD
Hannah STEEL
Daniel STEEL

1

Chrisnukkah

The Christmas tree and chanukiah shared the living room, like attendees at an interfaith event who don't understand each other but are willing to try. The tree was ten times bigger, its wide, leafy arms bedecked in white baubles and glass globes cradling artificial snow in slanted heaps. The familiar decorations were brought down from the loft each year: a glazed, ceramic heart Hannah had made at pottery class; a cloth robin that Daniel had bought at a school jumble sale; and little wooden apples that Chris had found in a craft fair, a secular choice as he was sensitive, always, to the fact that this time of year wasn't easy for Miriam.

Knowing what to put on top of the tree was an annual problem for her: an angel, too Christian; a star, likewise. So this year she'd opted for a glass bell. She liked it. But it was an unpopular choice with her kids.

'Who has a glass bell on top of a Christmas tree?' Daniel liked to pose his objections as rhetorical questions. Miriam was always surprised when her usually mild, lanky son became irate, as if there was more to him than even she realised.

'Only we would,' said Hannah miserably, always happy to emphasise to her mother that they were marginalised and deprived. Beneath the dark curls scooped up messily on the top of her head, her face scowled. Hannah was magnificent at sulking – downturned mouth, thunderous stare, creased forehead – and could change the atmosphere of a room in moments. Her usually pretty face twisted itself into fury.

Miriam had managed to keep Christmas, an uninvited guest, out of their house, when the children were young, as they were oblivious to the national celebrations exploding around them. She and

Chris would take them to his parents on the day, shifting the festivities to their home rather than hers whilst also not depriving Maureen and Ian of enjoying Christmas Day with their only child and his family. It worked well for many years until the kids grew older and became more conscious of what their friends were doing. Hannah, especially, felt it:

'Everyone else has Christmas trees and turkey and presents and we don't.' She folded her arms in protest. 'It's so unfair.'

Living as they did in the Midlands, with few Jewish people around, it seemed cruel to exclude them from the day of festivities and so gradually, sneakily, Christmas crept into the Steel household. It started discreetly: the first year Miriam bought a trendy metal tree that looked like a giant coat hanger coerced into a spiral; she decorated it minimally. The next year, the tree was wooden but the kids weren't satisfied with that either, deeming these attempts inadequate. They knew when they were being fobbed off. Besides, Christmas wasn't meant to be subtle or arty or nuanced. It was supposed to be shiny, brash, kitsch, gaudy and unapologetic. The siblings stood together for support against the injustice of it, knowing their rights.

The next Christmas the family graduated to an artificial tree and finally, some years later, they settled on an agreeable solution: a real Norwegian spruce, its fresh woody scent filling the house. Miriam had to admit that she liked the smell. Daniel would take the kids to the local garden centre to choose one and smuggle it into their home, like an interloper, bound in nylon netting which he'd cut, allowing the branches to spring open and unfold, spreading their limbs like a passenger being gratefully released from a packed aircraft, disorientated by its new surroundings.

But of course it didn't end there. The kids demanded the lunch too: the turkey, trimmings, Brussels sprouts (even though they disliked them, they still wanted them: it was like inviting Aunty Ida to their simchas, despite no-one really enjoying her company). Then bread sauce, cranberry sauce (no, chraine wouldn't do: too inky, too beetrooty, not traditional enough) roast potatoes and gravy as well; but Miriam put her foot down on that bizarre invention, pigs-in-blankets. She'd never had gammon or ham in the home, not because she thought for one moment that she'd be struck down by a thunderbolt if she did, but because it was simply alien to her. She knew that Chris sometimes sneaked off for a bacon butty in the university canteen, but she turned a blind eye to it when he returned home: ignoring the piggy smell on his breath, his shiny lips and the look of satisfaction and delight on his pork-stuffed face. After all, he did so much for her.

So her pigs-in-blankets surrogate was beef sausages wrapped in cabbage leaves but the kids weren't pleased. They knew that, once again, they'd been cheated.

One thing Miriam had learned about children: whatever you did, it was never enough; and if you gave in a little, you would end up giving in more.

Having relented on the tree and lunch, presents were their next target: but these gifts couldn't be modest or wrapped in secular striped or floral paper. They had to have ribbons and mistletoe, holly and reindeer and there had to be tags attached to the gifts. So many conventions, so many ways of fitting in, so many opportunities for not getting in right. Hannah and Daniel felt that their mother, unlike their friends' mothers, never got Christmas sorted, and they never stopped reminding her of the fact: Tilly's mother had an inflatable Santa in the garden; Joe's dad always dressed up as Santa; everyone's parents left out milk and a mince pie for Santa and a carrot for his reindeer.

After years of her experimentation and alternative solutions meeting with resistance, Miriam succumbed and gave in.

So this was where they were: a Christmas tree ('Think of it as pagan,' Chris said, helpfully) and on the sideboard the chanukiah, ready to be lit, its nine multicoloured candles looking like an advert for a Pride event. It stood on a foil-lined tray which Miriam had covered with dreidels in every size and material, and gold chocolate coins. She couldn't get Chanukah ones in this area so these had Santa Claus and robins embossed on their shiny surfaces. When the children were young, Miriam had given them a small gift each night: some coloured pencils, toys for the bath. Hannah and Daniel received them politely, their faces false-smiling, clearly disappointed by the meagre offerings.

Miriam had a Jewish drawer filled with candles, dreidels, kippot and Jewish books, cards and toys, which she'd amassed over the years. She liked to open it and see the familiar objects spilling out, shining up at her, but then she also felt bad about it: should Judaism be kept a drawer? Should it not pervade the house, the family, their lives, rather than be confined to a small space and allowed out occasionally?

Miriam knew that in north London, her sister Ruth would have be giving her kids more substantial gifts. When the rabbi had said the previous shabbat in shul that one shouldn't try to make Chanukah compete with Christmas as it is only a minor, albeit a significant, festival Ruth felt guilty and modified the presents she'd been intending to give, trying to find a compromise between the rabbi's wisdom and her children's happiness.

Bach at the Steel household, after presents and lunch, the family sang carols in the living room. Daniel played the piano and they had 'Away in a Manger' and 'Jingle Bells'; they ate too much chocolate and played Trivial Pursuit. Then Miriam said it was time to light the chanukiah. She liked it when Christmas and Chanukah overlapped. The celebrations melted unto each other. Everyone had something to enjoy, and she felt less uneasy about it.

Lighting the candles on the chanukiah that her bubba Rivka had given her, Miriam sang the bracha and then they all joined in with Ma'otsur.

With the tree lights shining and the Chanukah candles glowing, the room was full of warmth. 'Let's sing some Hebrew songs,' suggested Miriam, so they did: 'Yerushalayim shel zahav', 'Hava Nagila' and 'Hatikvah', all of which Miriam had taught her kids as well as Chris, although he struggled with the guttural 'ch'. He hummed when the words were too hard. She knew that the three of them were joining in for her sake and noticed that they didn't sing them with the same gusto that they had the carols. Miriam felt that she was defending Chanukah, protecting Judaism, fighting its corner, making room for it in her home. The children were always teasing her for saying that everyone was Jewish: 'Did you know, kids, that Daniel Radcliffe's Jewish? Scarlett Johansson? Sarah Jessica Parker?' No, she thought: Judaism has survived persecution and discrimination for centuries and it's still here. It is robust. It is self-protecting. I need not worry about it.

'Seriously, Mum. You probably think the Pope's Jewish,' teased Hannah.

'Well,' replied Miriam, smiling, 'he does wear a kippah.'

They watched TV and played games, Hannah taking copious photos. Miriam knew that they would soon be on Instagram and Facebook and that the north London family would see the tree and the gifts and disapprove, but she let it happen. This was the way it was, she thought: imperfect. She had to accept it. She'd be relieved when the day was over, although she knew that the tree would stay until 6th January: 'It's traditional,' said Hannah. 'It has to stay up for twelve days or else it's bad luck.'

And all the time, Chris had his arm around Miriam, was smiling, was warm. She remembered when they'd first met at university, both reading English ,and how she'd liked him at once: tall and gangly, his eyes grey and benign, his manner sweet and slightly awkward. Self-effacing. He exuded goodness.

They started dating and soon, inevitably, they discussed religion.

'You know I'm Jewish?' she said. They were lying on a grassy bank, dotted with daisies. A swan was gliding down the river, followed by three cygnets, the disappointingly plain children of a glamorous mother. Miriam rested her head on Chris's chest.

'Yes,' he said, stroking Miriam's long dark hair. 'Is that a problem?'

'Not for me. What are you? Religion wise?'

'Lapsed C of E. My parents took me to church but I rebelled when I was thirteen and never went again.'

'Did they mind?' She liked it when Chris stroked her hair, her cheek, with his large, soft hands. He was clearly a man to trust.

'No. They accepted it. Would your parents mind me not being Jewish?'

'I don't know. I haven't told them yet but you know that my children will be Jewish, don't you?'

'Oh,' said Chris, lifting his mouth to kiss hers. 'So we're having kids now, are we?'

They laughed and she tickled him.

'You should be so lucky.'

But, in fact, she felt that she was the lucky one: to have someone like Chris, who was clever without being pretentious, kind but not needy, reliable, good fun. She was happy with him. He left gifts for her outside her student door: a book of poems by Keats; a posy of wild flowers he'd picked in the meadow; a poem he'd written her that was earnest and sweet.

She felt – knew – that they were deeply compatible.

'So he's on the same course as you?' said her mother, Evelyn, when Miriam rang to tell her that she was going out with someone.

'Yes. We're both studying English.'

Miriam thought: it will be the third or fourth question. Her mum would want to make it seem as if she wasn't curious as to whether he was Jewish or not but of course she was bursting to know.

'In your year?'

'Yes, same as me.'

'And he's from London also?'

'No, from the Midlands.'

'Lovely. What's his name?' She hoped for Nathan Fiedelmayer or Moses Makinsky.

'Chris Steel.' And there she had her answer in two words. Not Jewish. Miriam knew that her mother minded but pretended not to.

'No, he isn't Jewish,' Miriam said unnecessarily, because she wanted to say it herself and not try to conceal it. 'But he's lovely.' She was angry with herself for adding that and anyway, it didn't matter how nice he was. He could have built an orphanage in India and saved a species of dormouse from extinction: it still wouldn't make him Jewish.

'That's great, sweetheart. Bring him to meet us, eh?'

Evelyn sounded disappointed but she didn't want to be disappointed. She wanted to be liberal, tolerant, broadminded but she knew that she wasn't really any of those. Because one daughter had married in, would it matter if the other one married out? She had a 50% success rate so that was quite good, wasn't it? Would that mitigate the disapproval from the family? She could just imagine Ida's face. Her mother Gretel wouldn't be happy. Thank goodness Harold's bubbe Shlossy was no longer alive: baruch ashem.

'Miriam's dating someone and he's not Jewish,' she told Harold at dinner that night.

He froze, a forkful of salt beef near his mouth. 'Who?'

'Miriam. Your younger daughter.'

Harold had one ambition: to find peace; but he'd never managed it. Living in a house with three women had been an utter nightmare. At any given time, someone had a period, or was expecting a period or was recovering from a period. The only thing worse than having a period - and the moodiness and bad skin that accompanied it – was not having one. As his daughters started going out with boys (and Miriam was especially productive in this area) a late period could only mean one thing as far as they were concerned, but to him it was just another example of his family never being punctual. 'Jewish time,' he called it. As they were consistently late for everything else - shul, shabbat meals, school - why should their periods be any different?

Harold was fed up with the bathroom being filled with feminine items: tampons, tissues, earbuds and balls of cotton wool like little clouds, all designed to plug orifices and absorb liquids. How he'd longed for a son: a nice, uncomplicated, non-menstruating male with whom he could kick a ball and share a beer, someone who would recover quickly if things went wrong and wouldn't remember it – or allude to it - for the next ten years.

But no, he had daughters and even though they'd left home, they still drove him meshugge. There was always something going on: a crisis, a problem that he had to know about and hopefully solve, someone else's mess to clear up. Someone's hairdryer or heart was broken, or they needed money - 'Do I look like a cashpoint machine?' - or they needed comforting. He dreamed about being on a desert island: palm trees, the water lapping upon a golden shore, silver fish arching from the sparkling sea….

'So what do you think, Harry?' Evelyn was there, on at him.

'About what?' He put the salt beef reluctantly back on his plate.

'Oh you are so irritating. About Miriam having a non-Jewish boyfriend, that's what.'

'What does it matter? As my father used to say, we're on the earth and then we die. As long as she's happy.'

'Right. So even if the boy's an axe murderer, as long as they're happy, that's fine.'

'Axe murderer? Who said such a thing? Your imagination!' Golden sands, lapping water…

And so Miriam had brought Chris to dinner.

Chris looked from one guest to another and tried to remember everyone's names. Ruth and Simon were there, Harold and Evelyn, and of course they had to have Morris (bachelor brother of Evelyn, who survived any awkward social event by telling Jewish jokes which he led himself into by starting 'So…' and avoiding eye contact). And Harold's widowed sister, Ida, whose philosophy was, 'I've had a crap life so why shouldn't you?' Luckily, Evelyn's parents, Israel and Gretel rarely went out in the evenings these days, so there were two fewer people to appease.

Miriam pushed Chris into the dining room of her parents' house like a mother firmly coaxing a reluctant child down a slide.

'This is Chris,' she announced.

Chris, who looked thinner and paler than normal, as if he'd suddenly lost weight, courage, and all self-confidence, nodded politely.

'Good evening everyone. Thank you for having me,' and he held out some flowers for Evelyn.

'These are for you, Mrs Green,' and she took them from him.

'So sweet. Please call me Evelyn. Do sit down. This is Harold, my husband -'

'Long suffering,' added Harold. 'Pleased to meet you.'

'- and his sister, Ida,' (Ida put her head on one side and shrugged) 'and Miriam's sister Ruth and her husband Simon,' (did she say that with special affection or did Miriam imagine it?) 'and this is Morris, my brother.'

Chris sat down and looked nervous, as if he were going to be tested on their names later. 'Good evening, everyone.'

The atmosphere was tense.

'So…' said Morris, 'Moishe says to his friend, Hymie, "What do you think? I came home to find my wife in bed with my best friend." "That's terrible," says Hymie. "What did you do?" "I made myself a cup of tea." "You made yourself a cup of tea?" says Hymie. "What about the man in bed with your wife?" "Uch," says Moishe. "He can make his own tea." '

Miriam and Ruth laughed (they adored Uncle Morris) but no-one else did. They'd heard the jokes too many times before.

'Shush, Morris' said Evelyn. 'We're going to light the candles now,' and she passed a spare yarmulke to Chris. Miriam had explained to him about the blessings on the candles, wine and challah, so he was prepared, but he listened intently to the Hebrew, as if they were speaking in an undecipherable code. The little hat sat uncomfortably on his curly hair, like a boat on choppy waters, unable to settle.

Evelyn started to serve the meal - undercooked roast chicken as usual for shabbat - and everyone tucked in, managing to eat and speak at the same time. Chris was impressed: in his family, one did one or the other. Not only were these people able to converse but they did it across the table, to the people on either side of them, all at the same time, so that verbal arrows were shooting in every direction:

'Chicken's nice, Mum? Did you add lemon this time?'

'Yes. I thought we'd had enough of garlic.'

'Pass the potatoes round.'

'So Daniel, you study English like our Miriam?'

'You'll never guess who I saw? Only Gerry Ratowski. Over six feet tall now and married.'

'Gerry Ratowski? You're kidding me. Now that's a name I haven't heard for a while.'

'What? Can't be? You got the contract? Mazal tov!'

'Yes. He's married. Two kids.'

'So you like books, like Miriam?'

'Kids? Gerry? Pass the veg.'

Chris' eyes darted around the room, wondering when he was expected to respond and which question he should prioritise, waiting politely for a pause to arise. It never did. But the atmosphere was convivial, everyone friendly apart from Ida who shot him a few death stares.

Evelyn had one fear in life: that someone may not have eaten enough. She'd made three puddings: lokshen, fruit salad and a dairy-free sponge pudding (Ruth and Simon didn't mix milk and meat). She darted backwards and forwards to the kitchen, clearing plates, bringing more food, making sure that no-one went hungry. Guests didn't leave her home after a meal; they staggered out, bloated and heavier than when they'd arrived, undoing their zips and buttons, gasping for air.

'The broccoli's nice,' Ida muttered snidely to Evelyn. 'I like it raw.'

'Did you hear what she said to me?' Evelyn asked Harold later when they were in bed.

'Hm?' Harold muttered, just dropping off. 'Who?'

'Your sister, Ida. She said my broccoli was raw. I know how to cook vegetables, thank you very much. How dare she say it was raw?'

'Leave it,' said Harold, putting a conciliatory hand on his wife's arm. 'Let it go, will you?'

'Anyway, what did you think of Chris?'

'Who's Chris?'

'Your daughter's new boyfriend. He's tall, nice manners. Very quiet.'

'He's got two eyes, a mouth and a nose, and he breathes. What else is there to say?' Harold tried to sleep again. Palm trees, white sand…

'She could have found a Jewish boy tall as a lamp-post who had nice manners also. Nothing against him but it just makes life easier.'

'Nothing makes life easier,' said Harold, drifting off again. 'It's a headache from the moment you're born till the moment you die. Tsores and nothing besides. Good night.'

Miriam's experience at Chris' parents' home couldn't have been more different. His mum wore a floral apron over a plain dress and blushed coyly when she spoke, as if she was embarrassed by herself. Chris' dad was in a three piece suit and had shaved especially for the occasion, leaving his skin pink and shiny.

'Good of him to wear a suit for our first meeting,' Miriam said to Chris later.

'No. He wears a suit every day. He has one for gardening, one to put the bins out and another for handiwork.'

Maureen was petite, and looked uneasy about taking up any room at all. Ian was taller, but also managed to look bad that he was occupying space which could have been used by others. Miriam thought that they were the opposite of people who are comfortable in their own skin.

Whereas lunch at the Greens' house had been noisy and lively, this was near silent, the clock on the mantelpiece ticking like a metronome as they ate. Maureen served them roast lunch (Chris had warned her against pork so she made beef with huge Yorkshire puddings, boats drowning in a gravy sea) and there were only occasional comments, 'The meat's turned out nice,' or 'Anybody want more potatoes?' Pudding was trifle, which Miriam ate out of courtesy, though she was quite full. The blancmange and whipped cream sank to the pit of her stomach.

After lunch, they played Chinese chequers and dominoes and Ian showed Miriam his raspberry canes. Miriam found Chris' parents warm and modest, although some of their traditions were alien to her: net curtains in Ian's shed; the two-bar electric heater turned on although it was sunny; the way Maureen wheeled the already-filled plates in on a trolley. (In Miriam's family, you put bowls of food on the table and everyone helped themselves.) It was as if she were a middle-aged air hostess: she even kept her apron on after they'd eaten.

'Your parents are so sweet,' Miriam said when they had left and were taking the train back to university.

'Do you think so? They liked you, I could tell.'

'I hope so.'

'They did. They're quiet gentle people, a bit bemused by their academic son.'

'I saw that they only had a few books.'

'Yes. The Bible, the complete works of Shakespeare (which I won as a prize) and a nature guide to birds and butterflies.'

'How did they cope when you were at grammar school and clearly brainy?'

'A bit bemused but also proud. I'm relieved today went well. Now we've met both sets of parents.'

‘Well, one thing’s for sure,’ said Miriam, snuggling up to him. ‘Neither of us is going to go hungry at either house.’

Recipe: Evelyn's roast chicken

Take a chicken and stuff a lemon up its tochus.

Roast but take out when the flesh is still red raw.

If anyone comments, say, 'It's just a bit pink, that's all. Don't worry about it.'

Carve, saving the giblets and pupik for Harold (his favourite).

Avoid saying 'Who wants breast? 'or 'Are you a breast man?' to Morris, as it will only encourage him to tell inappropriate jokes.

Even if you don't say breast, Morris will still tell his favourite chicken joke:

'So...Moishe runs to the doctor and says, "Doctor, you've got to help me. My wife thinks she's a chicken!"

The doctor asks, "How long has she had this condition?"

"Two years," says Moishe.

"Then why did it take you so long to come and see me?" asks the doctor.

Moishe shrugs his shoulders and replies, "We needed the eggs." '

Serve with chraine and vegetables.

Wait for insult from Ida about the vegetables being crunchy.

Look out for signs of salmonella: nausea, vomiting, abdominal cramps or blood in the stool.

Phone NHS Direct.

Harold always thinks (but doesn't say): Israel is the home of milk and honey; ours is the home of milk of Magnesia.

Recipe: Maureen's Sunday roast

Put the vegetables on to simmer two weeks before the meal.

Wait until the water turns green.

Check for vitamins and nutrients. If there are any left, boil for longer to expel them.

Put the meat on a low heat in the oven for six hours until it's black and burned.

With beef serve horseradish; with lamb, mint sauce; with pork, apple sauce (but don't serve when Miriam is coming for lunch).

Enormous Yorkshire puddings are obligatory.

Plate up the food in the kitchen.

When ready, wheel in on a trolley and eat in near-silence.

Take two Rennies afterwards.

2

Ida

Ida was descended from a long line of matrilineal miseries. In some families, gifts are passed down through the generations: trousseaux, baby clothes, jewellery of sentimental value. But not in Ida's case: the women handed on a cynical detachment for life and a tendency to put it - and everyone else - down. There was a familiar family gesture: arms crossed under the bosom, head cocked to one side, raised eyebrows, downturned mouth and a shrug that had to be performed simultaneously. The great thing was that this bodily pose was transferable, transcending language barriers, and could be brought out at any time: when someone showed off their new-born son or daughter, announced an unsuitable engagement, or came downstairs in a never-before-seen outfit, seeking approbation.

This acidity only affected the women. Harold and the men in the family were untouched by, and sought refuge from, it when they could, viewing life more philosophically and refusing to be drawn into this whirlpool of negativity. They couldn't change the world so they accepted it and tried to escape when possible. The female shoulder-shrug meant: What do you think you're doing now? The male shoulder-shrug meant: What the hell do you want me to do about it?

Along with Ida's misery came martyrdom. 'Don't worry about me: I don't mind sitting in the dark,' or 'That's alright: I'll just have the crust', or 'I can have the burnt bit. That will suit me fine.'

The barbed comments and self-denial went brilliantly together, one feeding off the other symbiotically: the snide comments led seamlessly to victimisation, which in turn led smoothly to more bitterness. A perfect combination.

Not that Ida had intended to be like her morose forbears. As a child, she'd noticed this sourness in her mother Rivka and grandmother Shlossy, as well as her many aunts: no, she wouldn't follow suit. In fact, she was as determined to resist the trait, as the child of an alcoholic vows never to drink.

Observers were amazed to witness that amidst this moaning family was sweet, young Ida, with her long ringlets, deep dark eyes and rosebud mouth. She skipped rather than walked, sang rather than spoke, and smiled rather than frowned. She liked to gather posies of wild anemones from the nearby woods to bring home for her mother. Even when those around her scowled, she ignored them and kept her good humour. She knew that these women had hard lives – little money, minimal support, long hours doing menial jobs - and Ida determined to reject their natural bitterness about the world in general and the men who had either died, deserted or ignored them.

She developed certain talents: as well as singing and writing poetry, she learned to sew. Rivka taught her, but whereas she viewed it as a chore and a necessity, Ida loved it. She could take a bit of scrap material and make clothes for her dolly or later, for herself and others. She became so adept that she started taking orders and running a small business. That was how she met Ezra.

Ezra Pekofsky was a sweet young man with pink cheeks. He always wore a flat cap and luckily, one day, cycled over to Ida's workshop to order a gift for his mother.

'What do you think she would like?' asked Ida, pausing in her stitching of a hem and gazing up at Ezra. She liked the appearance of this clean cut, dark-haired young man, with skin that looked scrubbed. In fact, she blushed when she looked at him.

'I'm not sure,' said Ezra, removing his cap, and the bicycle clips that kept his trousers tight around his ankles. 'It's her birthday and I heard that you make pretty gifts. What do you recommend?' Now he felt shy, seeing this sweet girl with her long, dark hair, bent over her task.

'How about a shawl?' Ida held one up as an example. It was triangular, made of floral material and edged with lace.

'That looks perfect,' said Ezra. 'When should I collect it? I work at O'Leary's timber merchants not far away.'

'A week from today?' said Ida.

They smiled. That would give them a chance to meet again.

And they did, as well as many times afterwards. They liked to walk by the river, Ezra wheeling his bike, Ida's arm slipped through his, seeing how the water became a mirror to the trees above it, lowering their branches to kiss its silvery surface. And sometimes they went to a café for an ice-cream, Ezra carefully taking out from his pocket the coins he'd saved. Ida knew that by marrying Ezra she'd never be well-off but she sensed that she would be happy, his sunny disposition a welcome antidote to her bitter childhood.

When Ida met Ezra's family, his parents and younger sister, she could see where his cheery personality came from. They were just like him: smiling, full of fun, enjoying games and teasing each other: jumping out from behind doors and sprinkling the unsuspecting with water.

And when Ezra met Ida's family, he was amazed at how Ida had maintained her sunny outlook in that house of miseries. It was like a single rose growing among thistles.

When Ida and Ezra married, the wedding photographs were an amusing reminder of their special day and the very different families with which they shared it. Next to Ezra was a row of smiling, beaming faces, but beside Ida were a row of scowlers, the men looking resigned besides their furious wives.

Ida and Ezra worked hard: him at the timber merchants where, after some time, he became foreman; her with her sewing. She built up a large clientele of customers who were impressed with her fine attention to detail and her tidy stitching; and it was an ideal job for her, as she could work from home, combining it with looking after their two sons, Nathan and Aviv.

Ezra was thirty six when he was killed.

Ida was at home, sewing; the boys were at school; a meat pie was baking in the oven. Then came a knock at the door of their terraced house. Mr O'Leary, owner of the timber merchants, was standing there, his head lowered, his hat in his hand. Ida dropped her sewing on the floor; she knew at that moment that Ezra was dead.

'What happened?' she said, her body quivering with shock.

'Ezra was delivering bills to local clients and a lorry knocked him off his bicycle. I'm sorry, Mrs Pekofsky, so sorry for your loss.'

Ida ran to the school to collect her boys and then went to tell Ezra's family. It was the first time she'd seen their smiles fade.

The meat pie was burned.

To say that the next few years were hard would be an understatement. Ida stayed in the house and was financially helped a little by Ezra's parents (not that they had much to give), a little by her own (they didn't have much more) and also by Harold and Evelyn, who remained loyal to her throughout, helping her in whichever way they could.

Nathan and Aviv grew up to be great men but Ida, struggling to keep on top of her sewing, motherhood and the household chores, whilst simultaneously dealing with her own grief, became what she'd vowed never to become: sour. Now when she looked at the wedding photographs where there was a dividing line between Ezra's smiley family and her grumpy ancestors, she could see that she fitted in well with her side.

Over time, Ida became a real misery: cynical, dour. Her boys, endowed with the genes of their father, found their mother rather a dampener. On their achievements at school, their friends and later, their girlfriends, she was impossible to please. Nothing was good enough and she found fault in everything. 'What a girl: couldn't she have brushed her hair?' 'Are you seriously going out dressed like that?' and once, when her sons prepared a meal for her on her birthday, 'The potatoes aren't cooked. Who wants to eat them crunchy?' Undercooked vegetables were a particular bugbear of hers.

Nathan emigrated to the States where he had a family and a successful business. Aviv made aliyah, happily settled in a land where people were warm and friendly and could pronounce his name. The sons kept dutifully in touch with their mother and came to visit occasionally; but she wouldn't travel to see them. 'To sit on an aeroplane with other people coughing on me? What do I want it for?'

Most loyal to Ida were her brother and sister-in-law. It was their mitzvah, their duty, they felt, to look after her and include her in every family event even though her presence was like lemon juice curdling cream. Judaism emphasises tzedakah: you should be charitable. You should be magnanimous. Sometimes, when Harold became frustrated with his sister's ingratitude, he remembered the order in Leviticus to glean your fields, leaving the edges for others to harvest. Their rabbi had said that this was literal as well as metaphorical: don't take all the goods for yourselves and let others go hungry; and don't take all your family nachas and exclude people: share your good fortune with them. When the rabbi said that, Harold immediately thought of Ida.

Harold and Evelyn lived by the line in the siddur which read: 'May my life be a link in a chain of goodness.'

So Ida became what she'd always tried to resist: a nudnik. Life had shat in her face so she was entitled to. Also, it was in her genes so it came naturally.

Those who didn't know her story saw her simply as an old grump with a set face and beige clothes; but Harold and Evelyn, who knew how she'd struggled, understood better. They sympathised with her and, as they couldn't afford to be generous to her financially, were generous to her emotionally.

Miriam and Ruth saw this behaviour as another example of their parents' bottomless kindness. Ida was at every barmitzvah, wedding, shabbat meal and family gathering, commenting from the side-lines in her sardonic way, raising an eyebrow at everything that came before her. It was hard to be fond of Aunty Ida or to love her. Sandwiched between Evelyn's anxious fussing and Harold's phlegmatic detachment sat Ida, now grey-haired, overweight and frumpily dressed, a shadow of her younger pretty self. Having no daughters of her own, the female misery gene stopped with her; but she was never going to change. She didn't smile. Why should she?

That was Ida and if you didn't like her (and, let's face it, most didn't) tough luck.

Recipe: Ida's Fried Fish

Take whatever fish you have.

Mix it with matzah meal, egg and herbs.

Shape it into patties or balls.

Fry.

Eat.

Open all the windows.

Wash your clothes and hair.

Take the curtains to the drycleaners.

Ignore the neighbours when they complain. How's it your problem?

Recipe: Ida's stewed apple

Peel, core and slice some apples.

Don't add sugar or spice.

Boil into submission.

Eat them, tasting how sharp and acidic they are.

That's life for you: bitter.

3

Hallelujah bread

The search took place every Thursday evening after work: hunt the Challah. More difficult than finding the afikomen on Pesach or the proverbial needle in a haystack, Miriam would scour the bakery departments of all the local supermarkets, driving from one to another, seeking the elusive plaited bread. Her eyes would scan baskets and shelves of sourdough, wholemeal loaves, French sticks and baguettes like long yeasty weapons, round loaves and square ones but no luck at all.

Desperate, she asked at one counter. A woman dressed in white overalls and cap and looking more like a surgeon than a baker came to help her.

'Do you have any plaited loaves, please?' asked Miriam, having learned by now that the word 'challah' in the Midlands would get her nowhere.

'I'll just ask, duck.' She called out the back. 'Ethel, have we got any of that hallelujah bread?'

She came back to break the bad news. 'Sorry love. No. But we've got focaccia.'

It was at one of the last stops that Miriam had some luck. There it was, one lone loaf, in a polythene bag: mazal tov! Miriam grabbed it, carrying it like a treasured baby to the till. She knew that Ruth and Evelyn always had two challot but she was happy just to have one.

Back home, she waved it triumphantly in the air.

'I got a challah!'

And so that shabbat they lit candles, said the brachot on them, the bread and wine and the kids joined in, Hannah a bit sourly, Daniel quietly, but at least they were there, sitting together at the table, sharing the shabbat meal that Chris had cooked them: a lamb tagine with apricots.

Miriam concluded that it was certainly easier when the children were younger to lead them in Jewish ways but, as they grew more independent, it was becoming more difficult. Once Hannah and Daniel realised how few Jews there were in the area – hardly any at their school, apart from one with a Jewish grandparent, one whose parents were Jews for Jesus and another who wore a Star of David but had a tenuous Jewish connection – they struggled with the sense of being different and wanted – understandably - to fit in.

Miriam would lie awake at night worrying about this issue, which she seemed unable to resolve. How did she instil a sense of Jewish identity in her children without keeping them away from society? How did she encourage them to mix with children of other faiths or no faith and yet retain who and what they were? How could she help them to respect the beliefs of others whilst still defending their own?

Chris would stir from his sleep, sensing his fretting wife beside him.

'Mimi, love, it's okay,' and he'd help her back to sleep, placing his hand gently on her lower back which often helped to soothe her.

The problem was that religious quandaries arose almost daily. Miriam didn't want to keep her children out of school assemblies and isolate them (as she knew her Uncle Gerald did with his kids) so, of course, they knew all the Christian prayers and hymns and it wasn't uncommon for them to start singing 'Give me oil in my lamps, keep them burning' or 'Onward Christian soldiers' on long car journeys to London. Miriam didn't stop them: to do so would be hurtful to Chris. Even though he no longer went to church, these hymns were part of his heritage and, as he was so tolerant of Miriam's identity, she felt she had to be tolerant of his. Maureen and Ian understandably gave their grandchildren not only Christmas gifts but also Easter eggs and, again, Miriam didn't feel she could say anything about it. They'd never met any Jewish people and, although they were fond of their daughter-in-law, they didn't understand her strange customs. The first time they came to Chris and Miriam's home, they pressed the mezuzah, thinking it to be an ornate doorbell and were baffled by the fact that it didn't ring and no-one answered the door.

What Miriam tried hard not to do was to equal something English or Christian with something Jewish, as if they were rivals or weights on a scale. It was tempting to do so and redress the balance but her kids disliked it. If they said The Lord's Prayer, she wanted to say, 'Don't forget the Shema,' or when they buried their beloved hamster, Ginger, in the garden, they instinctively made a cross from sticks and Miriam wanted to say, 'Why not a Magen David? How do you know that Ginger was Christian?'; but she remained quiet.

These worries gnawed away at her. There was no-one in the family she could talk to. If she spoke to Chris about it, he'd be upset and feel that he was to blame or that she regretted marrying him. If she confided in Ruth or her mum, she could anticipate their response: you made your choice, Miriam. Stop moaning.

But Miriam did find support in her best friend at work, art teacher Mehreen. Coming from a Muslim background, she faced the same issues as Miriam: wanting to instil her own identity and sense of heritage in her children but also allowing – encouraging - them to integrate. Her husband Afzal and their two boys, Jamil and Taj, got on well with Miriam and family and they were good friends, often joining together for meals or summer picnics. One year they rented a cottage on the Welsh coast and had a great time together: walking on the beach, taking a tram up the Great Orme and siting on a cliff edge, eating fish and chips and watching the sun go down. It was good to be away from the usual dilemmas that dogged these women.

Ever since they'd left home for university, and then when Miriam went to do her Masters in the US, she and her sister had always rung each other on shabbat. Once Ruth was married to Simon and they'd become more frum, the sisters had to speak before lighting the candles, but when they were younger this wasn't an issue. No matter what tension there'd been between them during the week - and there had often been some - the sisters always upheld this tradition. It was their way of saying: you drive me crazy but I still love the bones of you.

'Shabbat shalom, Mims.'

'Shabbat shalom, Ruthie.'

The sisters had fought all their childhood. If there was an object they could squabble over, they did so: a wooden block, a toy, a doll, a book. The item was immaterial: if one girl had it, the other wanted it. There was fighting, screaming, tears, wailing and later on, they graduated to punching, scratching and hair-pulling. Evelyn was bemused: how come she could control thirty children (some with complex needs) in one classroom but not manage her own daughters? She'd thought that a three year age gap would mean that they would be friends but it hadn't worked out that way.

It drove Harold nuts. 'What's the matter with you girls?' he would wail. 'Just love each other, will you?'

But of course they did love each other (and hate each other and treasure each other and resent each other) and if Evelyn scolded them (it tended to be her, not Harold – he avoided conflict) the sisters then backed each other against the new opposition. You enemy's enemy becomes your friend.

'Don't speak to her like that!'

As Ruth and Miriam matured, they became quite different. Ruth was a star pupil, especially at Maths, and was often appointed to responsible roles at school: Class Monitor, Prefect, then Head Girl. At cheder, she was invariably the one chosen to light the first candle at Chanukah, given the a lead role in the Purim play and awarded the class prize. With her neat, short, dark hair and fresh, glowing skin, her appearance reflected what she was: decent, reliable, a follower of rules. She was that rare girl whom teachers and pupils all like.

Miriam watched this transformation of her sister from fellow fighter and rival to decent, mature person with some consternation. As Ruth was older, she was always the first to do anything and always seemed ahead. She couldn't catch Ruth up. With Ruth having secured her place in the family, school and world, Miriam sensed that she'd have to find another role: the first was taken. As Ruth was brilliant at Maths, Miriam was arty, loving music, art and, most of all, books. As Ruth liked to keep her hair short, Miriam let hers grow wild and long, flowing in dark, curly rivers down her back. Ruth started dressing smartly for school, shul and social life so Miriam favoured loose cotton tops, dyed jeans and chunky jewellery, covering her wrists in bangles and her fingers in rings. And whereas Ruth hung out mostly with Jewish friends through the youth club Maccabi and went on several RSY Netzer summer camps in Israel, Miriam had a mixture of friends from different backgrounds. For her gap year, Ruth went to a kibbutz in Galilee; for hers, Miriam went to teach in an Indian school.

They no longer fought the way they used to – screaming, squabbling – but the rift between them grew wider and harder to heal. Miriam felt that they were like two cyclists, starting on the same path but then veering off in totally different directions as time passed, occasionally knocking into each other. They both agreed that they wanted Judaism to survive but disagreed on how to do so.

If Judaism were a swimming pool, Ruth would be in the centre of it; Miriam was sitting at the edge, dangling her feet in the water, and Uncle Gerald wouldn't even be in the building.

When Ruth married Simon, Miriam was still at teacher training college, going out with Chris, and although the wedding day in the shul was a beautiful occasion, the events leading up to it caused much tension.

Ruth had six bridesmaids: Simon's two cousins, an old schoolfriend, two colleagues and Miriam (all Jewish) but she asked her schoolfriend Sarah to accompany her to the mikveh.

'Why not me?' Miriam asked her at one of their family shabbats, before the event.

Harold rolled his eyes at the ceiling and ate his wife's meal (recipe 82: chicken with sweet and sour sauce. Unfortunately, some of the quantities had been obscured by fat spots and so Evelyn had rather overdone the vinegar.) Here we go again…

'Because,' said Ruth carefully, Simon loyally beside her, 'you live so far away now and I didn't think you'd want to come with me.'

As Harold fought back bile, Miriam fought back tears. 'I'm still Jewish and I'm still your sister,' she said quietly. 'Even if you don't live in north London and don't go regularly to shul, you can still be proud of being Jewish. And I am. Judaism doesn't just belong to you.'

Chris put his arm around Miriam and felt awkward. He wanted to protect his girlfriend but didn't want it to look as if he were siding with her against her family.

'Sorry,' said Ruth. 'I didn't think it would matter that much to you.'

'So who wants more potatoes?' asked Evelyn.

Oy ya yoy, thought Harold. Couldn't there just be peace? For one week, dear Lord?

Ida shrugged her shoulders: in this family, the sisters squabbled and the mother couldn't cook. So what could you do about it?

'So…' said Morris. 'Moishe and Rebecca are sitting on a bench and a tarty young girl walks by.

"Hiya Moishe," she waves, waggling her fingers.

"Who's this?" asks Rebecca.

"My girlfriend."

Rebecca shrugs. Another floozy walks past and waves, waggling her fingers.

"Who's this now?" she asks.

"Hymie's girlfriend."

"Uch," says Rebecca, "our one's prettier." '

When Chris and Miriam married, soon after their graduation, it was at a registry office with a reception at a lovely hall nearby. Miriam wore a long flowing dress, not white, but multi-coloured, with gold threads and Chris wore blue trousers and a white grandfather shirt. Maureen (in a plain dress and hat) and Ian (in a new suit) didn't like what their son and Miriam were wearing but they were happy that Chris was marrying such a sweet girl. They were introduced to Harold and Evelyn, with whom they had little in common, but they were all civil and smiled politely for the photographs.

Ruth and Simon had Leah by then and she was a sort of bridesmaid in a floral dress and peonies around her head but Miriam and Chris didn't like the whole best man/bridesmaids/ushers business, feeling it all to be rather conventional and gendered.

Guests - Jewish, Christian, Muslim, Humanist - were encouraged to wear bright colours and the meal was vegetarian: salads, nut roasts, fruit. Maureen thought they could have done with some beef and Evelyn chicken: neither said a word but chewed the greens like there were goats. There was no top table - people sat where they liked on long benches but Morris somehow still ended up near Ida as if he were destined to be always near her. He tried one of his Jewish jokes:

'So…how is a Jewish mother different from a rottweiler? The rottweiler eventually lets go,' but as the other guests on the table were Catholic and Hindu, and Ida made it a principle never to smile, the punchline fell like a lead balloon, crashing to the floor.

After the meal, while a variety of coffees and herbal teas were being served (Maureen and Ian had never seen green tea before) there were speeches: Miriam spoke, and there were readings of poems - Buddhist, Jewish, secular - by various friends.

When Miriam thought of her wedding, she remembered it as a day of colour, light and love but she regretted that there wasn't more of a Jewish element to it. She'd tried in vain to find someone in the area to give them a Jewish blessing but it wasn't the norm in those days and she'd failed to arrange it.

Now when she looked back at the photos (she'd put hers and Ruth's in the same album with cover title: Two sisters. Two weddings) it gave her a level of discomfort. There were Ruth and Simon: the chuppah, its poles decorated with white roses and foliage; Rabbi Woolf's beaming face; Simon in a kippah and talit; Ruth in a beautiful white dress and veil. And then her own wedding: colourful, enjoyable but secular. Once again, she felt that Ruth had taken Judaism for herself and cut Miriam out.

So, she realised, your whole life, maybe eighty or ninety years, was determined by one decision you made. She thought about confiding in her dad. He was a loving father, caring and kind. She remembered when she'd had her appendix out, how he'd sat with her at the side of the bed, patiently, holding her hand. But he didn't like long, analytical discussions and if he felt one starting, he would say: life's hard enough without having to dissect it. Leave it! Let it go!

Although she and Chris were happy, and could talk about books, film, music, the kids, nature, politics, life, this issue about her Jewish feelings upset him. He was happy to join in with her on shabbat, go with her to Purim parties and seders, but if she tried to talk to him about her sense of isolation or her feelings of being edged out of Judaism, he took it as a personal criticism. He interpreted it as her saying that she wished she'd married someone Jewish and was living in Goldwell Hill. Was she saying that? No, she was trying to say that she loved him but that she also wanted to be part of the Jewish life that she felt excluded from. It was the only time they ever argued.

Sometimes she thought: I have gone from Green to Steel whereas Ruth has gone from Green to Gold.

Miriam did talk to Mehreen about it, in the school canteen. It was hard to be heard above the noise of staff chatting, pupils guffawing and crockery crashing. There was a tradition at Mounthill that if a pupil dropped a plate and it smashed, there would be cheering. It had long been the suspicion of the staff that kids were dropping them on purpose in order to receive the rousing adulation.

‘How can I show my family that I want to be part of this country at large but also be Jewish?’ she asked Mehreen. As usual, they’d both chosen salad.

‘I know what you mean, Miriam,’ she said. ‘It’s exactly the same for me. My siblings both live near our parents and are very involved with the mosque and yet I’m trying to integrate while also keeping my Muslim identity. I attend the mosque also.’

‘Exactly. It seems as if you have to be all in or nothing.’

‘Yes. And you either fail or succeed.’

‘But the funny thing is that although my sister’s more religious than me, someone really religious, we call them Orthodox Jews, would consider her barely involved.’

‘There’s always someone more observant. It all depends on where you place yourself on the line - which may not be where your parents want you to be placed. My mother would like me to wear the hijab, like my sister and sister-in-law do and I don’t want to. I dress modestly but in a Western way.’

Miriam smiled warmly at Mehreen. She looked at the dark-haired woman in front of her, her beautiful eyes lined in black, her skin smooth and brown.

It’s interesting, thought Miriam, that the only person I can talk to about my Jewish identity is a Muslim. Thank goodness I have her.

4

Morris

Morris knew that he was gay even before he could speak or walk. He'd never disclosed his sexuality to anyone in the family, not even Evelyn and Gerald. He didn't need to: he knew who he was and he feared their disapproval. As a toddler, his mother Gretel (maybe sensing at a deep level that her son wasn't like the other boys) would encourage him to flirt with girls: 'Look, Morris, there's little Betty.' 'Go and sit beside sweet Judith.' 'Isn't Rachel lovely?' but Morris would stare at their ribboned hair and pretty dresses and feel indifferent. It was like asking him to form an attachment to an ironing board or a pile of bricks: nothing there. But with boys: that was another story. They were gorgeous and divine. Morris knew that his preferences weren't acceptable, so he kept his desires to himself.

Although, at times he'd experienced real loneliness, he developed strategies for coping. He buried himself in his accountancy, working more hours than he was paid to and, when his colleagues returned to the warmth of their houses, wives and families, Morris stayed in the office, toiling until the sky grew dark and thus reducing the time he'd need to spend alone at home. Once there, food and whisky provided some comfort, although his weight gain bothered him and he would stare, horrified, into the mirror at the large, double-chinned man who glared back at him. His stomach became so rotund that he could no longer suck it in for photographs: it simply refused to cave in. He wondered if anyone would ever find him attractive. He couldn't blame them if not.

The extended family also provided some solace and he was especially fond of his nieces and their children. It was a double-edged sword, of course. In a way he belonged but he wasn't at the heart of the family: an uncle, not a father; a brother, not a husband. When it came to gatherings, he was aware that he was never on the top table but seated at what he called, in his head, the 'pick and mix' or 'miscellaneous' table: singletons, misfits, those with hearing aids and wheelchairs, or sometimes dementia, and always his sister's sister-in-law Ida whom no-one could convince to crack a smile. He'd even tried two of his best restaurant jokes on her:

'So…Moishe goes into a restaurant and says to the waiter, "I'm missing my mother today. Bring me something that my mother used to make and give me some warm words of advice, like she used to say."

The waiter returns with some gefilte fish on a plate and places it in front of Moishe.

"Thank you," says Moishe, "but what about the warm words of advice, like my mother used to say?"

The waiter leans forward and whispers in his ear, "In this restaurant, son, I wouldn't eat the fish." '

No response, so Morris tried his other restaurant joke:

'So…the waiter comes up to a table of Jewish women and asks, "Is anything okay?" '

Not a smile: nothing from Ida. She didn't recognise herself as one of the women in the joke.

Morris' coping mechanisms involved avoiding eye contact, conflict and difficult conversations, while telling jokes. He never needed any introduction: he led himself in with the word 'So…' followed by a pause. The joke didn't have to fit in with the topic being discussed but if it did, so much the better, and if some people laughed and others didn't, then so what? At least the tension was diffused. Time had passed and hopefully with some levity.

These jokes – usually with Moishe and Hymie as the central characters – had carried Morris through his life. They weren't just for public consumption: he often lifted his own mood by recalling some of his favourites, either hearing the words in his head or saying them out loud. Many a fellow driver had been bemused by the sight of Morris in his Morris Minor, ostensibly talking to himself and tilting his head back and laughing as he recalled Moishe and his various antics. Not only did Morris know all the words to hundreds of jokes by heart (and he always used the same words): he could also visualise poor Moishe, struggling through life, his wife betraying him or his mother driving him meshugge:

'So…Moishe rings his mother.

"How are you, mother?" he says.

"Fine."

"Sorry," says Moishe. "I've dialled the wrong number." '

He identified with Moishe, not in every detail, but he was also put upon, his life often a disappointment:

'Mummy, Mummy,' says Moishe after his first day at school. 'I can write already.'

'I don't believe it,' says his mother. 'The child's a genius. What did you write?'

'I don't know. I haven't learned to read yet.'

Morris didn't just chronicle Moishe's issues with his mother and unfaithful wife but also his escapades with the tailor, the waiter and others besides.

'So...Morris is at the restaurant and he says to the waiter, "There's a fly in my soup. What's it doing there?" The waiter leans over to look: "Breast stroke, I think." '

'So...Moishe is fed up with his meagre income so he summons up all his courage and says to his boss, "I want a raise. Or else –"

"Or else what?" growls his boss.

"Or else I'll work for the same amount," says Moishe miserably.'

Morris found the jokes funny but he also felt Moishe's pain: an imaginary ally. He sometimes cried for Moishe: tears of empathy and humour. Life wasn't easy for him or for Morris. They were brothers on their knees, groping in the dark and trying to survive. He was laughing with him, affectionately. Both men were lonely but they also struggled on, stoically, never gave up.

Some nights, Morris lay in his bed and wept until the sheets were sodden with tears. In the darkness, he felt his isolation and shame more acutely although, once the morning came, he often felt a bit lighter in mood and made himself laugh with one of the jokes from his mental catalogue. Although he was close to both Evelyn and Gerald (meeting up regularly with his sister in Jewish contexts and his brother less often in secular ones) they didn't provide him with much solace. Sandwiched between two straight, seemingly-balanced people didn't help him to feel better about himself.

Morris had been in love just once: through friends he'd met Cecil, Jewish, a doctor and gay: what more could a person want? Cecil had mild green eyes, soft skin and a humility about him in spite of his good looks, impressive intellect and compassion. Morris couldn't believe his luck and the feeling was mutual. Cecil liked Morris' humour (thank goodness he enjoyed the jokes) and could sense that beneath the big body and twinkling eyes was kindness personified.

It was good luck and gave Morris the chance to tell one of his favourite jokes:

'So…Hymie says to his mother. "I've got good news and bad. The bad news is that I'm gay."

"Okay," says his mother. "What's the good news?"

"I'm dating a doctor." '

Together they cooked cholent and chopped liver, drank rather a lot of whisky, and fell in love with each other's minds and bodies. But whereas they had so much in common, there was one big difference between them: Cecil was ready (surprisingly, given his gentleness) to come out to his family and the world and publicly declare his love for Morris. Morris, however, was more reticent. It was too late. Coming out, he argued, was something you did in your twenties, not sixties. He'd missed his chance.

'But do you deserve some happiness, too?' asked Cecil. They were sitting in Morris' living room, lamb baking in the oven, each holding a glass of white wine, having the same conversation they'd many times before. 'All around you, people have mitzvahs and nachas and you toast their good fortune but you've never been able to allow yourself to be happy. We have one life, Morris. Isn't it time?'

Morris shook his head and then downed his drink. 'I just can't. The disapproval from everyone would be more than I can bear.'

'From whom?'

'Oh, my sister and her husband and the children and then Ida, she's my sister's sister-in-law with a face like sauerkraut and I just can't do it. They see me as the family bachelor, asexual. Can't we just carry on in secret?'

'Are you ashamed of me or yourself?'

'Of me,' said Harold. 'So Moishe goes -'

'No, I don't want to hear about Moishe. I want to hear about Morris and his quest for happiness. One short life, Morris, remember – that's all we have.'

They ate their meal in a frustrated silence and from then on spent most of their time arguing, not loving and it was always about the same topic.

'I want someone proud to be with me,' said Cecil, running his fingers frustratedly through his salt and pepper hair. 'To be happy to introduce me to their family and friends. I've spent my whole life tiptoeing about. Not anymore.'

'Sorry,' said Morris. 'I can tell jokes and run a firm of accountants but I can't come out.'

Sadly the relationship came to an end.

Morris resumed his old routines: working late at the office, coming home and eating and drinking more than he knew he should, putting on more weight, attending shul, going to family gatherings and just being good-natured Morris: joining in, cracking jokes.

‘So…Moishe is found by police on a kerbside and he’s crying.

“What’s the matter?” asks the policeman.

“I’m an eighty-year-old widower whose young girlfriend wants to make love three times a night.”

“So, what are you crying for?” asks the policeman.

“I can’t remember where I live.” ’

Morris missed Cecil with a physical pain in his chest and when he received a text from the same mutual friend who’d introduced them to tell him that Cecil was now in a civil partnership with another GP, it nearly destroyed him. He was at Harold and Evelyn’s at the time and they were just about to start their shabbat meal: undercooked roast chicken, Evelyn’s staple. Someone had given her a recipe book for her wedding - 101 Ways to Cook a Chicken - and she’d worked her way through it many times, but she didn’t do so systematically, page by page, meal by meal. She liked to move around the book randomly and give everyone a ‘lovely’ surprise.

Morris put his phone away (there was a no-devices-at-the-table rule here) and drank some water to cool his burning heart. He’d had his chance with Cecil: he’d blown it. He’d never enter into a relationship again.

‘So,’ said Morris, accepting a plate of chicken and vegetables from Evelyn, ‘Moishe gives his wife Rebecca a negligée for a present so she thinks that she’ll show her gratitude by putting it on. She goes to change, but the material is so sheer that she thinks she’ll trick him, for fun. She comes down naked. “What do you think?” she asks, doing a twirl.

“For that price,” says Moishe, “you’d think they could have ironed it.” ’

And in that way, Morris buried his own homosexuality within the heterosexual marriage of Moishe and Rebecca, giving the impression, without actually lying, that he, too, was straight: the accepted narrative was that, sadly, he'd just never met the right girl.

Recipe: Morris' evening meal

Order a takeaway, Indian, Chinese or Thai.

Drink whisky while you wait for it to be delivered.

When it arrives, drink whisky with it.

Have a nightcap: whisky.

Slump in a heap.

Throw the cartons away the following morning.

Feel ashamed.

Vow to lose weight.

Recipe: Gefilte coffee

Make a cup of black coffee.

Float a slice of carrot on the top.

Recipe: Gefilte fish

Put a carrot slice on a koi carp, like a yarmulke.

Watch him float religiously through the water.

5

Shylock and shyness

'So I'll have to teach *The Merchant of Venice* then, after all?'

'Yes, Miriam. It's the only choice, I'm afraid.' Hilary, her Head of Department, buttoned her navy jacket and tried, as always, to find a balance between compassion and authority. 'We can't do *Romeo and Juliet* at GCSE as they'll have done it in Year 9; the only other option is *A Midsummer Night's Dream* and we feel that works better with Year 7s, what with the fairies and the magic.'

Miriam remained quiet.

Hilary did too. She was older than Miriam, mid-fifties, divorced, childless, devoted to her work. 'I know that it wouldn't be your first choice but you'll teach the kids the background and context to the play and I'm sure they'll understand. There are texts I don't like either – I can't stand *Animal Farm*, as you know, but I still have to teach it.'

Miriam smiled politely. She liked Hilary, admired her management of the department and her dedication to work but there was a blind spot when it came to religion or family issues. She remembered when Daniel had tonsillitis and she and Chris had struggled with work and childcare; Hilary hadn't been overly sympathetic. As long as you were working hard, she was fine but she didn't respond well to obstacles or bumps in the road.

All through her career, Miriam had been open about being Jewish but had protected herself by avoiding teaching texts that she knew could lead to possible antisemitic or ignorant comments from the kids. Anne Frank was fine (although the kids did keep writing about *The Dairy of Anne Frank*) but she avoided teaching *Moonfleet* because of the diamond merchant, Krispin Aldobrand,

Oliver Twist because of Fagin, and *The Merchant of Venice* because of Shylock. She had some ambivalence about the stream of Holocaust fiction and films that was coming out. Partly, she felt that it was vital for youngsters to know the horrific facts and understand where hatred can lead to, but there was something uncomfortable about making merchandise out of something so horrendous. The suffering of people was being used for entertainment. Was that right?

Her mum, Evelyn, used to introduce herself to each new class by saying, 'I'm Mrs Green and I'm Jewish,' so that in a sense she got there before they did. She also said that she felt she was an ambassador for Judaism: if the kids in later years remembered her as warm and empathetic, they'd always think positively of Jewish people, but if they didn't like her, it would be the opposite. It was an enormous responsibility. If she ever heard anything untoward, such as a boy whose friend had denied him a sweet saying, 'You're so Jewish,' Evelyn would take him to one side and calmly explain that not only was his stereotype wrong, it was also unacceptable. She felt it incumbent on her to deal with it, not just let it go.

'I totally get that,' said Mehreen when Miriam first told her the story. They were eating lunch together in the school canteen, as they often did. They even tended to choose the same food: soups, salads, the vegetarian options.

'That's how I feel,' she said. 'Because I'm the only Muslim teacher here, I feel like the banner carrier for Islam. I don't mind when the RE department ask me to come into their lessons and talk about my faith or go on school trips to the mosque - and I know you've done the same, Miriam, with Judaism - but it's quite a burden, isn't it?'

'Certainly is,' said Miriam. 'You have to choose your words carefully. They think that I represent all Jews but of course there's such a wide range of beliefs and practices.'

'Exactly. We're only one example, not all examples.'

Thank goodness she had Mehreen, thought Miriam, clearing her tray. She completely understood. When either of them had an issue, be it at work or home, they consulted each other, a barometer of feelings. They faced the same issues: should I ask for a day off for Yom Kippur / Eid? Am I over-reacting to a situation? And they each had their issues with Mr Fletcher, Deputy Head, disliked by staff and pupils alike for his snide comments. 'Let's hope today's lunch doesn't contain pork,' he said to the women once as they entered the canteen; and another time, 'I don't suppose you ladies will be attending the staff Christmas lunch,' whereas in fact they both always did. His little jeers never seemed bad enough to complain to the Head about but they made the women feel uncomfortable and it was vaguely insulting: did he see their religions as preoccupied solely with diet? Did he think that was all they were about?

And so Miriam began to teach *The Merchant of Venice*. She told the class at the outset that she was Jewish (following her mother's lead) although most of them already knew as she sometimes did assemblies at Chanukah and on National Holocaust Memorial Day. She was careful to explain the context first: how in sixteenth century Venice, Jews were discriminated against and there were very few opportunities open to them, so that was why they often turned to moneylending or usury. She photocopied a helpful article on it. And all the time she was teaching it, she liked to show its relevance to today, bringing in articles on racism, antisemitism, homophobia, transphobia and discussing other issues around prejudice and discrimination while always linking it back to the text and Shakespeare's words. They weren't hard connections to make.

The class she was teaching was Year 11 Set 2 so quite able, but it was a group which was rather imbalanced. There were a few loud confident pupils and some very quiet ones - and then there was Lucas. He worried Miriam. He said little, sat alone, and had few friends at school. Whereas most of the pupils (especially the girls) were smartly dressed, their uniforms shiny, their hair washed, Lucas looked scruffy: his shoes were dirty, his shirt creased and stale, his hair unwashed. On mufti days, while the other students chose their clothes carefully, he looked shabby. He had acne on his cheeks and forehead and he never made eye contact with anyone, teacher or pupil.

In the classroom, Lucas worked quite well, only occasionally staring at the sky through the large window but mostly completing his work. The standard was quite good, although he didn't always answer the question being asked. His spelling and punctuation were weak yet he often made interesting observations or took an angle different to the other kids. He didn't just regurgitate in essays what Miriam had said: so many children's essays read like transcripts of her words but Lucas added in his own ideas. The previous year, they'd been studying *Jekyll and Hyde* and Miriam had been explaining that the name Hyde was a pun as he was the side that Jekyll tried to conceal but when Miriam marked their work, Lucas had written that Hyde was a pun on animal hide, reminding us that he was a beast. He added that when Hyde paced the room, it was like a lion in his lair. Excellent, wrote Miriam in the margin: you're developing your own ideas, Lucas. Well done.

However, getting Lucas to do his homework and hand it in on time was nigh-on impossible. He didn't care how many detentions and warnings he was given: you simply couldn't extract the essays from him. His parents were called in for a meeting with Miriam and Hilary. The parents looked scruffy. The dad avoided all eye contact when Hilary spoke to him as she always did, firmly, calmly, and stared at the ceiling lights; they seemed defeated by him.

'You're the teacher,' said the mother, bitterly. 'It's your job to make him work, not ours.'

And so the class edged tentatively through *The Merchant of Venice*, both sides uneasy. It was different from studying *Romeo and Juliet* where the kids giggled over the romantic bits and always defended the teenagers' forbidden love: this was Miriam trying not to be defensive, allowing the pupils to express their ideas; but she sensed that they were uncomfortable as they knew that this subject was close to her heart. They liked Mrs Steel: with her long, curly dark hair and colourful clothes, she was fun, interesting, warm, but she was also strict about work and didn't stand any nonsense. She had boundaries, but she was genuinely interested in what the pupils had to say and write.

And then something extraordinary happened: Miriam realised that, whereas she was trying to be objective in criticising Shylock, 'His idea of asking for flesh is horrendous, surely?' the kids were defending him, 'What other option did he have, Miss? Isn't he behaving like that because of the way he's treated?'

When they reached the speech: 'If you prick us do we not bleed? If you tickle us do we not laugh?' the kids erupted into a dynamic discussion about homophobia, transgender issues, racism, modern day antisemitism; she no longer needed to remind them that the play was relevant to today: they could see it for themselves.

The following day Lucas approached her, shyly, and drew from his rucksack some crumpled sheets of paper. When she read them later, as usual, he'd ignored the question asked, and had failed to use any quotations; but there was a rant about injustice, and then he ended with the line: Mrs Steel (spelt wrongly), you do not need to apologise (also spelt wrongly) for being Jewish (ditto). U are amazing. (smiley face)

When she saw him next lesson, she handed back his work with a positive comment at the end and he blushed, deeply.

'That's because you're a great teacher and the kids can trust you,' Chris told her later when she recalled what had happened. They were clearing up after dinner.

They hugged in the kitchen and carried on with the chores.

One of the many areas of their lives that they shared was their love of books, often pointing out interesting passages to read to each other, finding relevant quotations, one reading a novel that the other had just finished and then discussing it.

Chris was struggling with his research, a book on Shakespeare's Children. His idea was to write an introduction about Shakespeare's own children, Susanna, Judith and Hamnet and then slip over to the depiction of children in his plays. So far he'd written four chapters:

Chapter One: Childlessness: *Macbeth*, *Julius Caesar*

Chapter Two: Lost Children: *The Tempest*, *The Winter's Tale*

Chapter Three: Difficult or Destructive Children: *Coriolanus*, *Romeo and Juliet*

Chapter Four: Disobedient Children: *King Lear*, *Othello*

After that, he was struggling. It was often the way with Chris: his initial enthusiasm fizzled out.

Some sample chapters had been sent back by the publishers with two anonymous readers' reports. Both basically said the same thing: interesting subject, scholarly work, lacklustre feel. 'This book,' said one, 'has a genuine contribution to make to Shakespearean scholarship but it needs more vitality.'

He had to have this book published for the Research Excellence Framework in the spring. His Head of Department would be critical of him, were it not completed. And his chances of getting a personal chair, well, they were zero without another publication. His previous book had been published before the children were born. No coincidence. This next one needed writing. Seriously.

Part of the problem was that Chris was naturally quite cheerful and he found it depressing to focus on such dark matter.

That morning he'd been working on *Coriolanus* and the destructive child:

'I saw him run after a gilded butterfly; and when he caught it, he let it go again; and after it again; and over and over he comes, and up again; catched it again…he did so set his teeth and tear it…'tis a noble child.'

He enjoyed teaching the students and didn't even mind the admin too much but sitting on his own in his study working on academic analysis when he could rather be with Mimi and the family: it took a self-discipline which he didn't always have. Sometimes in the evenings, when the kids were with friends or in their rooms, he and Mimi would clear the kitchen table and work at the same time, her marking and preparing, him writing. That helped but if he could hear the family in the garden on a summer's day, he couldn't force himself to go to his room. It was like leaving a party to sit in a monk's cell.

'Emphasise the joy of children more,' advised Miriam. 'It all sounds so heavy. What about Polixenes in *The Winter's Tale*: 'He makes a July day short as December;/And with his varying childness cures in me/Thoughts that thick my blood.'

‘You’re right,’ said Chris. ‘It needs more energy, more dynamism. I’ll get on with it.’

And so he and Miriam egged each other on. She also consulted him about ideas for school, ‘I want to teach a lesson on sonnets, old and new. I’ve got the Carol Ann Duffy *Prayer* and Empson’s which I think they’ll like. It’s a top set. Which Shakespeare sonnet would work best?’

And Chris would ask her to read his chapters and make comments. She knew that he sometimes found it hard to focus on his work so she, gently, urged him on.

‘Why not go and do an hour on your book, Chris, and I’ll get lunch ready?’

And in this way, they carried on dancing through life, helping and supporting, loving each other.

As Hannah and Daniel grew up, they became more defined and more different from each other in looks and in every other way. Hannah was more like Miriam, round-faced, pink-cheeked, feisty, outspoken but also easily hurt, tending to analyse and overthink. Daniel was thin, lanky, pale, gentle, quiet, bookish, more like his dad. When they were next to each other, Hannah looked alive, energetic, ready for a fight. Daniel looked anaemic, scared of danger.

Miriam noticed that at family gatherings in north London, Hannah was more extrovert, mixing with Ruth’s daughters and being quite loud. Daniel and David became closer, as if they sought refuge in each other’s sensitivity.

Harold liked to stretch his arms around his grandsons and hug them. They were great lads but quite delicate. When he’d dreamed of having a son or grandson, he didn’t envisage gentle boys like these. He had in mind large, robust blokes who were confident and didn’t bear grudges.

It was this closeness between the cousins that led Ruth to her idea.

They were at Leah's batmitzvah. An extrovert, self-confident girl, she sailed through the Torah service, reading her parashah with clarity and aplomb. She had the portion from Leviticus XVI about the sacrifices offered and she read about the goat who carried upon him the sins of the children of Israel. In her d'var Torah, Leah explained how the word scapegoat derived from this passage and how we sometimes make scapegoats of others, especially minorities. She was both eloquent and suitably serious.

At the reception lunch afterwards, at a beautiful hotel near the shul, tables were laid in stiff white napery and huge floral displays stood on stands. Swans carved from ice flanked the buffet. Miriam and Chris were on the top (family) table (Chris noticed again that he was the only non-Jew in the room) with Ruth and Simon, Harold and Evelyn, Gretel and Israel (Abie and Rivka had both passed away by now); the young cousins and family friends, twins Jacob and Saul. Of course Gerald and family wouldn't attend.

On the 'pick-and-mix' table were Morris, Ida and others in the miscellaneous category: a divorced cheder teacher who had helped nurture Leah; a spinster, a widower, and a sweet lady who'd decorated her wheelchair in silk roses for the occasion.

Over a delicious meal of salmon, new potatoes and vegetables with a selection of teas and coffee, the noise in the room was palpable: talking, laughter. Morris tried to unite the table:

'So…' he began. 'Moishe says to Rebecca, his wife. "Be truthful. How many men have you slept with?"

"Only you," said Rebecca. "With the others I was awake." '

Ida scowled. The others remained stony-faced but the lady in the wheelchair tilted her head back and laughed.

Morris was about to tell another joke, but then there were speeches; Simon, Leah and Rabbi Woolf.

In the car on the way home, Miriam and her family talked about the day.

'The dancing was fun,' said Hannah, her eyes bright.

'Would you like to have a batmitzvah, Hannah?' Miriam asked, tentatively. She'd been meaning to broach the issue for some time and now seemed the right moment.

'I don't know.' Hannah stared out of the car window at the trees and bushes that whizzed past. 'None of my friends at school do it although some have been confirmed.'

'No, but your cousin's just had one. I could help you with the Hebrew and Rabbi Woolf would support you, I know. Have a think about it.'

Hannah did think briefly about it but decided against it. The idea of her non-Jewish friends wearing their best clothes and sitting in a line, listening to her reading unfamiliar words was not appealing. She wanted to blend in, not stand out.

When Miriam rang Ruth to tell her of Hannah's decision, she heard her sister's usually friendly voice turn icy. 'You shouldn't have given her a choice,' she said. 'They don't know at that age what they want. You tell her, don't ask her.'

'That's not the way we parent,' said Miriam defensively.

'And there we differ,' said Ruth. 'Shabbat shalom, Mims.'

'Shabbat shalom, Ruthie.'

Miriam put down the phone and felt herself tremble.

Would Daniel be more amenable when it came to his barmitzvah? She hoped so, but she also hoped that he would do it because he wanted to, not just to please his mum or to compensate for his sister's refusal. It wasn't fair to expect him to do that.

Once again, Miriam slept badly, dreaming that Daniel refused to have a barmitzvah and her parents and sister disapproved. But it had to be his decision. She wanted him to choose to lead a Jewish life, not just follow in blind obedience. That would be in contrast to the way that she and Chris had agreed to raise their children.

She remembered years earlier there had been a school trip to an activity centre in Devon. It was optional and, although she and Chris pointed out the merits to Daniel, he didn't want to go.

'All that climbing ropes and assault courses. And I don't want to share a room with ten other smelly kids.'

'That's fine,' Miriam had reassured him. 'You don't have to go. It's your choice.'

Daniel seemed relieved but, as the trip grew closer, the others children's excitement was palpable; he changed his mind. He went and had a great time. But it had been his choice. Surely the decision to have a barmitzvah was the same?

6

Harold

As a child, Harold was surrounded by miserable women, bemoaning their lot, waving their arms in the air and nagging their husbands. The men reacted in a number of ways: some drank; others had affairs; some were made unhappy by it. It was Harold and Ida's father, Abie, who seemed to have the right idea: he was philosophical, detached, not willing to be brought down by the griping he heard about him. His wife Rivka and his Yiddish speaking mother Shlossy - who dressed like a man, smoked a pipe and threw out insults (she liked to group them in threes: schmerils, schlemiels and shmoks) along with her sisters and their daughters and what not, all went on about the lack of money and the list of chores to be done. But to Abie it was water off the proverbial duck's back.

'What's that got to do with me?' he would say or 'How's that my problem?' But his favourite reaction, on hearing someone else's woes, was 'So let his mother worry.' These three rotating phrases served him well and all conveyed the same message: it's your shit, not mine.

The great thing about this phlegmatic attitude was that it was multi-purposed. Once you adopted this blasé stance (and Abie seemed to have it off pat) it could be applied to demanding children, moaning wives and disgruntled employees alike, though there was a downside. It meant that he didn't really care, feel passionately, about issues or put his heart and soul into anything: nothing really mattered that much to him. It was as if he floated above life, detached from it, looking down on it.

Sitting somewhere between their mother's misery and their father's detachment wasn't easy for Ida and Harold. 'Two paths diverged in a yellow wood…' Ida was determined to take the happy route (although no-one who met her later could believe that) but Harold took the path of apathy that his father had already trodden for him.

Abie's father Isaac had started a company. Like many other amazing refugees, Isaac had arrived in this country with nothing other than the clothes he was wearing, a determination to succeed and a good business brain. He took a job polishing and repairing furniture and he worked hard for years, saving what he could until he was able to open his own import/export furniture business, which did really well. But whereas Isaac was driven, single-minded, ambitious, his son Abie had this indifference to life.

Abie joined the family furniture business but by now he was married to Rivka, who nagged him, and Abie developed a defensive shell around him: indifference. Under Abie's watch, the firm didn't do as well as previously and there were constant rows between Isaac and his son.

'You roll up late. You don't keep on top of the paperwork. What are you doing to our business, son?' asked Isaac, waving his hands in the air. In the background his wife smoked and drummed up her Yiddish insults about her lazy boy: nogoodnik, gornisht and blofer.

'Take it easy, would you?' said Abie. 'Life isn't just about work. It's also about pleasure.'

'Pleasure?' shouted Isaac. 'What's pleasure got to do with it? Do you think we are put on God's earth to have fun? Life's a hard slog, you provide for your family and then you die.'

These arguments were legendary and took place not just at home but also in the factory where the employees become used to the sound of rowing. They would be polishing furniture or wrapping it up for transporting, when shouting would come from the office as father and son vented their anger and asserted their very different takes on life.

Observing all of this was young Harold. He looked around him at the various options on offer as if choosing from a menu: the angry women; his driven, pent-up zaider Isaac; his Yiddisha-speaking, pipe-smoking, insult-throwing bubba Shlossy; his sweet sister Ida; his moany mother Rivka; and his laidback father, Abie. It seemed to Harold that Abie had the right idea. Life was short. Why not enjoy it? Yes, you had to earn a living but who needs a fortune? How many houses can you live in at once? How many cars can you drive simultaneously? When you've had one meal, can you really eat another?

So Harold joined the firm and continued in the laisser-faire ways of his father. The two of them worked well together after Isaac retired but the business went downhill. Father and son were slow to reorder stock, settle their bills and chase late payments. Furniture – chairs, chests of drawers, dressing tables, wardrobes - stood packaged and ready to go in the warehouse but weren't sent for ages, resulting in stress and a loss of income, as those who had waited too long would not order from them again and understandably took their business elsewhere.

The good news was that Abie and Harold developed a wonderful father-son bond. When they stood face-to-face, rotund tummies almost touching, they were mirror images of each other: bearded, ruddy-cheeked, twinkly-eyed. They would raise their shoulders, turn their hands outwards, palms facing up like synchronised swimmers, as if to say, so what does it matter anyway?

The other positive news was that the employees were happier with the atmosphere - now there were guffaws coming from the office rather than shouting - but less happy when the money started to run out and redundancies had to be made. Isaac watched from the side-lines, broken-hearted to see the shrinking of his empire; Shlossy never ran out of triads of Yiddish words with which to insult the men: bonditt, bummer and colboy. Rivka wasn't too impressed either but her Yiddish wasn't good enough to insult with and her English equivalents - twits, idiots and good-for-nothings - to describe her husband and son were too weak to have any real impact, lacking the punch of Shlossy's Yiddish.

Into this fractious family came Evelyn. Not conventionally pretty, she was short and had dimpled cheeks and a spirited manner about her. She'd been looking for a project for some time. A primary school teacher during the week and at cheder on Sundays, she lived at home with her family but felt restless, as if she hadn't yet embarked on life. She knew that she was good at motivating small children but wanted something bigger that she could drive forward. What or who could it be?

At a Jewish club for young singletons run by the shul, she met Harold. At first, she didn't think much of him: a bit overweight, bushy-bearded, fat cheeks and a casual approach to life; but the more they saw of each other they more they started to think that they could work together: two unlikely pieces of a jigsaw.

'Tell me about your work, Harold,' she said one Sunday as they walked through a local park. He'd collected her after cheder and seen how the children gravitated towards, and loved, her. She'd make a good wife and mother, he thought.

Blossom had started sprigging the trees and the sky was a cloudless blue canopy over their heads.

'Well,' said Harold, hand-in-hand with Evelyn, a stretch on his arm as she was so much shorter than him, 'my father and I run the family furniture business but it's not going that well.'

'Oh. Why?'

'Maybe it's our fault. My zaider Isaac put his heart and soul into it but my father and me, we like to enjoy life and not take it too seriously.'

By now, Evelyn had laid a rug on the grass and they were sitting there together. She'd brought them a bottle of pop and a punnet of strawberries to share. She thought: I like this man. He's sweet but he lacks a bit of oomph. I could coax him along.

'What about your teaching?' asked Harold. 'Do you enjoy it?'

'Oh I love it. To have the chance to engage young children and get them excited about books and art is wonderful. I hope to be a deputy head one day or even head of a school.'

'And I'm sure you'd like your own children?' Harold blushed at his own question. Was he being, uncharacteristically, too forward?

'Very much so. I'm the oldest of three so I'm used to looking after little ones.'

Harold thought: sweet Evelyn. Five foot nothing of fun and goodness and she loves family and children. What more could anyone want?

Evelyn thought: I could do worse than marry Harold. He's delightful and I could shoot a rocket up his tochus.

They were married in shul before their large family: the seamstress had to cut Evelyn's wedding dress down (she made curtains from the excess) and she looked sweet and radiant, her dark eyes shining out under a boyish haircut beneath the veil.

Some people sense the night before their wedding that they're making a terrible mistake. Harold and Evelyn felt the opposite. Although Evelyn could be anxious, she was also courageous and he knew he needed that. She felt that Harold was goodness itself, that he would be kind to her and that together they would make a good team. She was right.

At the wedding the congregants felt the same. They cheered and sang and, when Harold smashed the glass with his heel, there was whooping and applause. The big, bearded, carefree man and the short, nervous, ambitious woman were well-matched and everyone knew it. They feasted and danced until the early hours surrounded by love and approbation - apart from Shlossy who muttered Yiddish insults under her breath (pisher, momzer and putz) and smoked her pipe.

So Harold and Evelyn played roles within their marriage: she was a nudnik, he was non-plussed; and others (their daughters Ruth and Miriam included) accepted these as the truth, the whole truth and nothing but the truth.

But what no-one saw was that when Harold and Evelyn were alone in bed, or standing in their garden at night, watching the stars, their love was strong, serious and steadfast.

In fact, it was one of the happiest, most loving marriages ever to have graced this troubled earth.

Recipe: Rivka's matzah and butter pudding

Take some matzah and soak in milk.

Layer it with cream, sugar, sultanas and orange peel.

When the dish is full, sprinkle on more sugar and double cream.

Bake.

Serve hot or cold with clotted cream.

Have a coronary.

While you wait for the ambulance, say, 'I know I shouldn't but…' and have some more.

So what if you die? At least you'll die happy.

7

Ash Wednesday and dust and ashes

Miriam knew, when she applied for the job at Mounthill, that the school had a Christian ethos. Not a fan of faith schools, she'd have preferred to teach in a mixed school with Jews, Christians, Muslims, Hindus and those of all other faiths as well as those of none, but there wasn't such an establishment in the area so, rather bored with her last school, she'd applied to a new one where she knew academic studies were valued but there was also a range of kids.

Her interview was going well. She'd taught a creative writing lesson to Year 11s watched by Hilary. Now the latter was joined by Craig Fletcher, (Deputy Head with a penchant for gaudy ties – today's had the Periodic Table embroidered in a metallic thread as if a slug had crawled all over it) and the Head, Elaine Fairweather (Miriam thought Elaine Frosty Climate would have suited her better), a stony-faced, flat-chested, tall, spiky lady who spoke harshly, emphasising the consonants, and dressed always in only one colour: today it was lavender.

So far the panel had asked Miriam about her past experience, the schools she'd taught in, how else she could contribute to the school, what she felt was her weak point (being too sensitive) and her strong point (empathy), how she felt about setting in year groups and how she would support those with Special Needs.

The atmosphere was polite and cordial.

'Thank you, Mrs Steel,' said the Head, after Miriam had responded. 'Is there anything you would like to ask us?'

‘Yes please,’ said Miriam shifting uncomfortably. ‘I want to just mention that I am Jewish.’ Craig Fletcher stared at her as if she’d just said, ‘I have three horns and they light up at night.’ ‘In many ways I hope that’s an advantage as I’m happy to take Jewish assemblies if you like and go into RE lessons and talk about Judaism, as I did at my previous school, but I may have to have two days off a year for the New Year and for the Day of Atonement if they fall on weekdays.’

‘That’s not a problem,’ said Elaine Fairweather, coldly. ‘We have a Muslim teacher here who has to have a few days off a year.’

Craig Fletcher scowled.

‘Thank you, and also in terms of assemblies, I’d be happy to attend them -’

‘You would have to with your tutor group. It’s part of your contractual duties,’ added Fletcher.

‘- of course, but I assume that I wouldn’t have to say or sing anything that I didn’t feel able to?’

‘That’s fine,’ said Ms Fairweather as if it wasn’t really fine but she knew she had to agree with it. Secretly, she missed the old days, when the teachers were mainly Christian. Nowadays even those who had had religious childhoods were often atheists and anti-religion, and stayed silent during the hymns and prayers. Therefore, she could hardly tell the apathetic students to join in when their teachers didn’t. However, she knew the employment laws and was careful to adhere to them, with her head, if not with her heart.

And so Miriam got the job and loved teaching at Mounthill. She liked most of the kids and most of the staff and meeting Mehreen was a bonus: they became firm friends.

As promised, Miriam was happy to go on the annual trip to a synagogue and answer the children's questions: What is the eternal light? What do you do if it goes out? Why does a rabbit take the services? Is it true that Jews don't have birthdays? And she also took assemblies when asked to.

One Chanukah, she took a menorah in, lit it and sang the blessing. She asked: who knows why Jews light the candles for eight days and a boy's hand shot up:

'Because Jesus is the light of the world,' he said proudly and to the annoyance of his RE teacher, as they had 'done' Judaism the week before. Mind you, he was the same boy who wrote in an essay that all Muslims worship Alan. (Miriam and Mehreen had tears in their eyes when they heard that.)

Once, Miriam and Mehreen took a joint assembly on how Muslims and Jews had more in common than not and it went down well with students and staff alike. They ended with their arms around each other's shoulders. There were children there who would remember that visual symbolism for the rest of their lives.

Dutifully, Miriam accompanied her Year 8 tutor group to all assemblies, joining in with the hymns when she felt they were generic ('All things bright and beautiful', 'Morning has broken', 'The Lord's my shepherd' and other psalms presented no problems) but remaining quiet when she needed to. After a while, she discovered that recalling the words of the Shema in her head lasted as long as it took the school to recite the Lord's Prayer and that seemed a good solution. For the rest of her teaching career, she silently recited her own prayer while remaining respectful to others.

Twice a year, at Christmas and Ash Wednesday, the school went, en masse, to the cathedral: weaving through the town in a crocodile, much to the delight of tourists who snapped the occasion.

Miriam accompanied her group, answering their questions to the best of her ability and consulting the head of RE when she didn't know the answers.

Miriam enjoyed what she could in the cathedral: the stunning architecture, the beautiful stained glass windows, the organ and choir, and at Christmas time, the candles were lit and the stone pillars decorated in holly and ivy. It reminded Miriam of the chuppah at Ruth and David's wedding where the four posts were adorned with roses, jasmine and foliage.

But it was Ash Wednesday which Miriam experienced for the first time. The service was fittingly sombre and with its focus on morality and sin, it was reminiscent of Yom Kippur; but what surprised her was that, when the students were called up to get ash crosses drawn on their foreheads, she saw many non-religious children (especially girls) go up to have theirs done.

Walking back to school, in the dreary February half-light, she realised that they were wearing them as badges of honour, almost fashion statements, lifting their fringes to compare their markings. Miriam made no comment about it but it made her feel rather low. Some of them had clearly missed the point entirely.

She told her family about this at their next shabbat. Whereas Ruth, Simon and their children went every Friday to Harold and Evelyn, Miriam, Chris and the kids could only go occasionally, due to the five hour car journey, which was only possible if there were no plans for the following day and they could stay the night. (It became harder when Daniel started playing football on Saturday mornings and Hannah took a part-time job.)

'And they put ash crosses on their foreheads,' said Miriam. They were all there, the candles lit, the wine and challah and the table covered with a white cloth. Miriam always enjoyed being with her parents for shabbat: it felt warm and familiar. Chris had also become used to it. He ate, smiled politely and made a few comments but mostly remained quiet, happy because Miriam was happy. The five cousins were seated at one end of the table and got on well, although David was often shy, when in large groups.

'Rather like Yom Kippur,' said Evelyn, always somehow able to speak, serve everyone food and eat her own (she was on recipe 101 now: chicken with thyme) and make everyone feel at home.

'Exactly.'

'Nice veg, Mum. The carrots are so sweet.'

'Crunchy,' said Ida, her one contribution to the discussion. She knew that implying that Evelyn undercooked her vegetables really touched a nerve.

'I'd just never seen it before, the ash crosses.'

'I like it,' said Harold, 'every year when our rabbi falls down on the bimah. It shows such humility.'

'So…' said Morris, grateful to his brother-in-law for inadvertently leading him into one of favourite jokes. 'It's Yom Kippur and the Rabbi says, "Before you, God, I am nothing. I am dust and ashes." Mr and Mrs Feldman, who are wealthy donors to the synagogue, follow suit declaring, "I am dust and ashes," and the caretaker, Michael, joins in and declares, "I am dust and ashes."

"Huh," says Mrs Feldman, nudging her husband in the ribs, "look who thinks he's also dust and ashes." '

Miriam and Ruth laughed, Harold nodded his head and Ida scowled.

They were all members of the same shul. Whereas Harold and Evelyn were sporadic attenders, Ruth and Simon went, unfailingly, every Saturday morning, with the kids attending cheder on

Sundays. Ruth helped as much as she could, outside her work: organising the Purim party, volunteering to tidy the library, and taking stints in the Judaica shop. Simon, with his business knowledge, sat on the finance committee. Miriam and her children were associate members as they were only able to visit occasionally, while Chris was a friend of the shul. This made Miriam feel that she was at the edges of it, whereas Ruth and her parents were at its centre. If the shul was a book, she thought, her family were the text and she was the margin.

Rabbi Woolf was a large, genial man, bearded and kindly. He was happy to see any of the extended Green extended family when they appeared but he never shamed his congregants for non-attendance. He didn't approve of ministers (of any faith) drawing their congregants through guilt or humiliation: 'Surprised not to see you on shabbat,' or 'Long time, no see, stranger.'

He wanted people to attend because they were eager to and not because they felt obliged to. Popular with the community, he managed to address serious issues but also introduce levity. His wife and three boys were all on the chubby side and had the same pink cheeks as if they'd come in a job lot.

One Sunday, when they were staying with her parents, Miriam told a white lie. She said she was meeting an old school friend (Chris was taking the kids to Madame Tussauds and the Tower of London) but she actually went for an appointment with Rabbi Woolf.

'Come in, Miriam, dear,' he said, ushering her into his messy study at the shul. Books lined the shelves and also lay on top of others, books on books. Miriam thought that not only were some books commentaries on other books; they were actually lying on top of the books they were assessing. There was also a Spurs banner and a photo of him, his wife and kids on holiday in Eilat. Their beaming faces and wide girths filled the frame as if they were about to burst out from it.

‘How can I help you, Miriam?’ he asked when they were seated on opposite sides of the desk. He smiled genially. She wondered if he was ever irritable or sad or angry. He always conveyed serenity.

‘I chose a hard path,’ she began. He listened, waited, but didn’t speak. ‘Ruthie chose an easier way of life: Jewish husband, kids in Jewish schools, family, community. For some reason I made my life difficult. I love my husband deeply but being married to a non-Jew and living in a non-Jewish area is a daily struggle.’

‘Yes, I understand. Everything you do, you have to think carefully about, make a decision whereas for some it’s easier, they can take things for granted. But be careful you don’t think that everyone’s life is simpler than yours. We all have struggles and pain, wherever we live or what religion we are. You know, the Levys tell me the Cohens have the perfect life. The Cohens tell me that the Levys have. It is about perception.’

‘I know.’ Miriam fought back tears. ‘I thought that living in mainstream society but being Jewish would be easy but it’s not.’

‘No, it’s not. But you are brave, Miriam. You may have taken a hard route but you are doing well. You are a teacher, wife, mother, daughter, sister and wonderful member of our shul. We’re always happy to welcome you and your lovely family when you’re able to come.’

‘Thank you, Rabbi.’

‘You are leading your best life, Miriam. You are serving God in so many ways. What more can any of us do?’

And the tears rolled swiftly down Miriam's face. She wouldn't have been able to say whether they were the product of guilt, tiredness, emotional exhaustion or relief but she felt comfortable crying in front of the rabbi. He didn't move or say a word. He sat with her, focused on her, as she sobbed, gently edging towards her the box of tissues which he kept in the office for such occasions. His secretary had to buy him new boxes of tissues on a weekly basis.

Unembarrassed, he let her cry.

When she felt calmer, she dabbed her face with a tissue and felt her cheeks warm.

'Your life is a blessing,' he said quietly.

Then he stood in front of her and said: 'May God bless you and keep you. May God's face shine upon you and be gracious to you. May God's face turn towards you and give you peace'. Miriam said, 'Amen' and then and he recited it in Hebrew:

Yivarechach adonai veyishmerecha. Ya'el adonai fanuv elochu viyoonecha. Yishah adonai fanuv elochu veyasem lecha shalom

And once again Miriam said, 'Amen'.

When Chris and the kids met her in Oxford Street later, a tourist in the city where she'd grown up, Chris said, 'You seem calmer somehow, Mimi.'

She hugged her family.

'Shall we find somewhere to eat?' she said. 'What about Italian? We all love that.'

8

Gerald

I agreed to do my barmitzvah and that was that, as if I'd fulfilled the terms of my contract. I knew at the time that it would be my farewell to Judaism (although it's supposed to be the start of your adult journey as a Jew) and that I wouldn't be involved again. I found learning the portion easy and I performed, I think, with aplomb but it was a performance. I didn't believe in God – I never have – and I did it for my mother's sake. I don't think my father's that bothered but my mum is a conventional lady with a deep connection to her faith and I did it to please her. I can still remember how proud she looked that day.

I'm sorry that my abandoning of Judaism has hurt my mum. I take no pleasure in the fact that I have, in her eyes, let her down but hopefully the other parts of my life – my career as a scientist, my wife, Jenny and our children, Sebastian and Jo (we became parents later in life) – have given her some happiness, although I doubt it.

The truth is I believe that religion is load of nonsense. I don't mean one religion in particular, but rather all of them: burning incense, praying and bowing to someone who isn't there, refusing to open the fridge on shabbat in case the light comes on. If there is a God – and I highly doubt it – I don't think that he would want you to adhere to rituals like those.

People turn to these weird practices because they provide security and comfort in an uncertain world. I know many scientists who are religious – it's not my job that stops me believing. It's not even that I need concrete proof. Science is more nebulous, hypothetical and complex than people think. When laymen refer to 'the science' it makes me laugh. There is no singular science. There are always multiple possibilities. Scientists argue with each other all the time.

In my opinion, religion is responsible for many of the atrocities in the world: the Holocaust, the never-ending tension in the Middle East; Northern Ireland; Islamophobia; anti-Semitism; the treatment of the Muslim Rohingyas in Myanmar. How many more examples do you need? Wars, abuse, divisions, acrimony: everyone believes their religion is the right one and is intolerant towards others.

I have had many arguments with my family and friends over this but I believe that religion complicates and makes problems. Why do we need it?

I resent the way that schools in this country are either faith schools or the state ones are C of E. We took Sebastian and Jo out of RE lessons and school assemblies when they were children. I didn't want their heads filled with that mumbo-jumbo. I know that they found it difficult being withdrawn (they sat in the library and did their work) and I'm sorry that it upset them but we are the parents and we had to decide what we wanted our children being exposed to.

Jenny and I have always been on the same page in our anti-religious stance. I could never have married someone who wanted to go to a synagogue, church or temple. She was brought up in a weird so-called religious cult where the adults had sex with the children (they called it free love) and it was all ghastly. They worshipped a man who didn't deserve any acclaim. I don't know how Jenny is so stable, although years of therapy have helped her.

My stance has never gone down well with the family. Mum, Gretel, wanted me to be involved with the shul. My sister Evelyn couldn't understand my point of view: she sees Judaism as our precious heritage which we have a duty to pass on, like Chinese whispers. For years, she kept inviting me to Jewish family gatherings and I refused to go. I was happy to see family in secular settings – picnics, holidays – but I wouldn't be involved in religious events. I turned down invitations to barmtizvahs and weddings. After many years, Evelyn eventually gave up asking me.

Morris is less concerned. I don't think he has a deep belief if I'm honest. I think he attends family events for the social side. He's lonely and he likes the idea of belonging. That's fine if it suits him but I don't really like the idea that we use religion as a comfort or community. I think you should believe the words that you say. I'm not willing to say things that I don't mean. If we did that in other areas of our lives – in a court case, for example - that would be seen as dishonest so why is religion any different? I can't bear hypocrisy.

My dad's not bothered either. He's not a great joiner-in but my mum has given me much grief about it and it has caused a rift in our relationship. She was a great mother when the three of us were growing up: warm, empathetic, encouraging, but that was when we toed the line, knowing no other way. We went dutifully to shul and cheder, did out bar and batmitzvahs and were obedient. Evelyn continued to follow the desired path but Morris with his sexuality and me with my anti-religious stance did not do as we were meant to. We were disappointing. Mum worries about what others will think and say.

She was indefatigable in her pursuit of the issue. Each time we saw her, there would be pressure: why don't you go to shul? Will Jenny convert? Why aren't you raising your children as Jewish? Why won't you attend family Pesach or Chanukah parties? She sent the children gifts at Chanukah and New Year. There's never been any respect given to my point of view or an attempt to listen to it.

It was as if there was nothing else for us to talk about, so when Jenny and I did visit my parents, that was all my mother would raise. As Jenny is not Jewish but as anti-religion as me, this made the atmosphere unpleasant and therefore we stopped going. Jenny felt unwelcome. Evelyn has graciously accepted our views. But my mother's like a dog with a bone.

It's such a pity. She didn't ever connect with Sebastian and Jo and ask them about their sport and their many hobbies or ask Jenny about her work as a nutritionist. As they wouldn't lead a Jewish life, she wasn't interested in them. I am very sad about it but I won't be coerced into a view that I don't have. That is religion by manipulation rather than choice.

Sebastian and Jo are in their twenties now. They are lovely people – Sebastian is in IT, Jo is a cellist - but they don't know their family at all, really. They both have partners, Sebastian is with Hatty, Ruth with Jess, both non-Jewish, but they would barely recognise their own cousins if they met them in the street.

The rift is a great shame but I won't ever be bullied into changing my views.

I've always argued that religion is divisive and our family demonstrates that exactly.

9

Evelyn

In their childhood home, it was made clear to Evelyn that Morris and Gerald had the brains and would have shining careers and that she should marry and have children. That, after all, was what her mother had done. Although those family aspirations were ones that Evelyn shared, they were not her only dreams for, as long as she could remember, she'd wanted to teach. It started when she was very young, lining up her teddies, dolls and brothers and giving them instructions and tuition. The toys were better students than the boys: silent and still, they never answered back.

From this, she graduated onto cousins and, at family gatherings, Evelyn would invariably be the one ushering in the youngsters and teaching them songs and rhymes, having fun but also keeping them in check. As she was not much taller than them, they had the feeling that she was one of them but also the one who was in charge of them.

As Evelyn's mother Gretel lavished all her attention on Morris (whilst simultaneously worrying about him), and Gerald (about whom she worried less) this gave Evelyn freedom. Morris was always overweight, sensitive, shy and there was a sense that he wasn't interested in girls. Whereas Evelyn would talk openly of her fears, 'Mama, I'm worried about going back to school tomorrow after the holidays,' Morris kept his hidden. Gretel felt that there was another side to her elder son, a side that he kept concealed.

Gerald was less secretive, less complex, but he was strong-willed and there were some conflicts at school. Once Gretel was called in by the teacher to discuss Gerald's dogmatic manner after he had voiced his opinions rather forcefully, even to staff. One young trainee teacher was humiliated when Gerald rather rudely pointed out her mistake on a test paper.

Gretel's husband Israel was a psychiatrist (who refused to retire). He'd heard such twisted, dark stories in his working life that it seemed to him that his own children were abnormally normal. It was no use Gretel trying to talk to him. He spent his whole day listening sympathetically to others and didn't really want to hear any more problems when he got home. Instead he took refuge in the garden where he grew vegetables of gigantic proportions. His courgettes and tomatoes were especially impressive. Each year he grew horseradish for the seder plate; it was so strong that even the hardiest men had tears running down their swollen cheeks.

If Gretel said to him, 'I'm worried about Morris,' or more rarely, 'I'm worried about Evelyn or Gerald,' he'd wave his hand as if shooing away a fly and say one of two things: either 'That's totally normal', or 's/he'll grow out of it.' As one of his clients, to give an example, had a fetish about goats and spent most of his time scouring the hillside for a suitably bearded 'bride', Morris' slight shyness, Gerald's inflexibility, or Evelyn's anxiety about her forthcoming exams seemed wholly insignificant; instead he lavished his attentions on his wonderfully non-verbal vegetables, watering, tending and even talking to them. No wonder they grew so large.

'He cares more about his cabbages than his own children,' muttered Gretel, who was left to raise the kids alone. Evelyn was flourishing at school, popular and sociable; Gerald (apart from his intolerance towards others) was achieving highly; but Morris concerned her. He was eating far too much and had such a sweet tooth: he could polish off a plate of lokshen pudding before it had even cooled. He didn't seem to have many friends, either: other children liked him but he didn't have a best mate and wasn't invited to many parties.

But then Morris discovered Jewish jokes. Someone gave him a book for a Chanukah gift; he loved it, and gathered more jokes wherever he could find them, building up a collection. Being blessed with a good memory, he stored them in his mind as a squirrel stows nuts in his cheeks. At first, his jokes were tame; only later in life, as his confidence grew, they became a bit naughtier.

His mother was his principal audience. She especially liked the ones about mothers and grandmothers showing off about their amazing offspring, perhaps recognising herself in them:

'So… three mothers are sitting on a bench.

"My son's a doctor," says the first lady.

"Uch, that's nothing," says the second, "mine's a barrister."

"And what about mine?" said the third one. "Only sixteen and already helping the police with their enquiries." '

And Gretel would throw her head back and laugh aloud. Through these performances, Morris honed his craft: always starting with 'So…' and leaving a slight pause before continuing, therefore building suspense, telling them in the present tense and making them as short and pithy as he could. Others soon heard of Morris' joke-telling skills and he started getting invited to parties, though more as a clown than as a friend.

Gerald was not really keen on the jokes and found them a bit silly: there were more serious things to think about such as pollution, the environment and global politics. Evelyn watched all this with interest. She loved her brother Morris but couldn't help feeling that beneath the laughter there was pain. He stood on his own, spouting jokes, but not really connecting with anyone. As he was three years older than her, it helped her to define who she wanted to be. She had no desire to be standing at the front, performing. She wanted to be at the centre, belonging and engaged.

While Morris and later Gerald went to university, Evelyn went to teacher training college and loved it. It was an easy decision to teach primary, amidst the children, rather than secondary, poised, Morris-like, at the front of the class, detached. Some trainees do better at the academic side than the teaching practice, others, vice-versa, but Evelyn excelled at both. She was bright and outgoing, the children instinctively knowing that she was trustworthy and good but that she also meant business.

With men, Evelyn seemed less successful. She attended the shul they'd always belonged to and had many friends; but no man seemed to take to her in particular. She wondered whether she was too short, too plain, too self-confident. And then she met Harold. Here was someone she could love, be loved by, and also help. Her own career was going well, and she could support him at the same time. They would be a team of two.

After Evelyn married Harold and they had their own flat, Morris also moved out of the family home. And after Gerald left, Gretel was lonely. She did some voluntary work and helped in the shul library, but she felt neglected by Israel who, after long days listening to other people's tsores, came home and lavished the love and care on his giant parsnips that Gretel wished he would lavish on her. While the vegetables flourished, Gretel shrank.

Recipe: Shlossy's Borscht

Take some bunches of beetroot, a carrot and an onion.

Peel and put in a pot with stock to boil.

Watch it, irritably, with your hands on your hips.

When it's cooked, cool and mix with eggs and lemon juice.

Serve hot or cold with a dollop of sour cream.

Argue about whether it's Romanian or Ukrainian.

Watch everyone's lips and tongues turn purple and then insult them in Yiddish: khloeye, khnyok and klazer.

Throw the pot and bowls away: they can't be used again.

10

Passover and takeaway

Whatever else was happening in the Green family, they always came together for seder. It might not always be on the first night for, if that fell on a week day, the Steels couldn't travel down and back to London in an evening: so they'd unite on the first Friday or Saturday that they could. If they were lucky, Passover would fall in the Easter holidays. Each year, when Miriam got her black academic work planner (September to July) the first thing she checked was when Pesach fell and whether or not it was in the vacation. Depending on the results, she either sighed or whooped.

For Ruth and Miriam, Pesach meant family. Harold and Evelyn would prepare the room, erecting a makeshift table next to the usual one (they put the youngsters down that end). The cousins always had bets on who would get the table legs between their knees and who would be asked to read the part of the simple son. Collapsible chairs brought in from the garden; white cloths spread over the two tables, (although one could still always see the dividing line between them); glasses polished till they gleamed; extra crockery (white china with a single green leaf printed on each rim) and cutlery that had been left by Abie and Rivka (both had passed away) had to be brought down from the attic each spring, packed in its cardboard box with newspaper padding for protection.

There was anticipation in the Green house each year and Miriam always felt it, even as an adult. She imagined that was how Christians felt about Christmas: tingling, excited, can't wait. When she and Ruth were young, they always had new white dresses for Pesach and their dark hair was brushed by their mother until it shone.

This year Passover fell on a Saturday so Miriam spent that morning getting the kids and their luggage ready. Hannah and Daniel liked seeing their cousins (although they found the seder a bit long) and there was always another family there too, with their twins, Jacob and Saul. For the last couple of years, she and Chris had employed a local lady, Donna, to clean their house once a week and to keep an eye on it when they went away. Although they lived in a semi, their neighbour Mrs Mcintosh (a kind old lady who always gave the children a few pounds at Christmas) was elderly and housebound so they couldn't ask her.

As they were packing the car for their long drive, Donna arrived.

'Oh thanks, Donna,' said Miriam, a bit flustered. 'If you could just do the curtains, morning and evening and clean the bathroom and kitchen while we're away that would be great. I've left your money on the table.'

'Okay love.' Donna stood in the doorway, arms folded. She had peroxide blonde hair, a pierced nose and a lopsided smile on a crimson-lipsticked mouth. She cleaned at the school where Miriam worked: that was how she'd found her. Donna was chatty and so Miriam tended to ask her to clean when they were all out or else she'd regale them for hours with tales of her wayward children and the many failed relationships from which they had been conceived.

Hannah and Daniel were already in the car, plugged into devices and resigned to the lengthy trek. Chris was packing the boot.

'Going to London again?' asked Donna, leaning against the lintel as if the house were hers.

'Yes. Remember I told you that we are Jewish and have an annual celebration where we share food with others. It's called Passover.'

'Oh yeah,' said Donna, smiling in recognition. 'We do the same in our house but we call it a takeaway.'

It took a while to seat everyone in the dining room but it was achieved at last. Harold sat at the head of the table, ready to lead the seder; Evelyn was beside him, near the kitchen so that she could pop in and out. Next to Evelyn was Morris and beside Harold, inevitably, was Ida. Miriam and Chris, Ruth and Simon, Rachel and Jonathan completed the circle and at the other table were the kids: Daniel and Hannah, Leah, David and Abby, and Jacob and Saul.

Once again, Israel and Gretel had sent their apologies. Evelyn was hurt by it. She knew that they were elderly now and it was all too noisy for them; but she couldn't help feeling that her dad was not really interested in them anymore and that her mum was dissatisfied with her children: her gay son, her granddaughter who'd married out, acerbic Ida. Evelyn always took her parents some seder pastries on the day but it didn't stop the disappointment.

She'd accepted by now that Gerald and Jenny would never attend anything Jewish. Gerald said that it wasn't just about Judaism: he despised all religions. In theory, she was fine with it: it had to be their choice. In practice, it still stung. She couldn't understand why they wouldn't come. No-one would make them say or sing anything if they didn't want to but it was about family, about belonging, about coming together. Surely that mattered? It felt selfish that he wouldn't bend a little but trying to persuade him was like trying to push a steamroller through mud. She had given up asking as it simply led to arguments.

Evelyn remembered the seders of her childhood as lovely warm affairs, the faces of the children illuminated by the candles like a painting by Joseph Wright of Derby. She and her brothers would join in and take their part to read (Gerald even used to sing 'Ma Nishtana' at that stage, before he rebelled) and the atmosphere was sweet and benign.

Now each of the tables had its own seder plate, which Evelyn had prepared with maror, shank bone, burnt egg, parsley and charoshet. There were boxes of matzoth, kiddush wine for the adults and grape juice for the kids, as well as jugs of salt water. Each place setting had cutlery, a linen napkin, a wine glass and a Haggadah. They were all slightly different editions, so finding the right page presented some issues. There was also a name plate designed by Evelyn and, on the reverse side, your role in 'Chad Gadya' for later. (She gave David the part of water: all he had to do was a gushing sound.)

It was noisy, with greetings, chatter and laughter.

'Love your top.'

'Thanks. How's your new job going?

'Stop it. It's mine.'

'Are you free for a weekend get-together? Let's look at our diaries.'

'Are we having macaroons afterwards?'

'Right,' said Harold, thumping the table genially but definitively. 'That's enough kvelling. Are you ready to begin?'

Everyone cheered and so he started.

Miriam squeezed Chris' hand beneath the table. He squeezed hers back. He'd had a snack beforehand, having learnt his lesson many years previously at his first seder. On that occasion, the pre-dinner proceedings had taken over two hours and he had become faint with hunger. Turning to Miriam, he'd whispered, 'Are we going to eat soon?' and she'd reassured him with the words, 'Yes, we're about to have hard-boiled eggs in salt water.'

Now, many years later, he knew what to expect and enjoyed it. He'd become used to the delayed food, being the only non-Jew in the room and he was even accustomed to Ida's death stares which, being affable, he returned with warm smiles.

'We start with the handwashing,' said Harold, 'which I will do on everyone's behalf.' He recited the blessing and off they went, filling their glasses with wine or grape juice when he told them to, lifting them high and saying the bracha together: *Baruch atah adonai eloheinu melech ha'olum beray peree hagofen. Amen.*

It was the one night of the year when Harold was clearly in charge: Pesach meant a lot to him and he knew that he had to assert himself (although it didn't come easily) in order to control the unruly mob. Tonight they mostly complied during the service, only the kids calling out when the maror was too strong, Evelyn's charoshet too sweet, and the famous Hillel sandwich not everyone's favourite. They read around the table (Miriam was pleased to land her favourite part, 'The mountains skipped like rams, the hills like lambs,') and although Ruth was worried about it, David took his turn, albeit in a soft voice. Abby sang the 'Ma Nishtana' with gusto and clarity and Harold included the children: Daniel was the wise son, Hannah the wicked, Jacob the dull son, and Saul the one who didn't even ask a question. When the time came, Leah was asked to open the door for Elijah. They dipped their fingers in their glasses to denote the plagues and, if the kids got a bit too noisy, Evelyn gave them one of her glares.

'So...' began Morris when there was a gap. 'Moishe would only eat either chopped liver or charoses. Not both. Otherwise he'd have charoses of the liver.'

No response so he tried another one.

'So…Bagel-maker Moishe Getz wants to belong to a club where no Jews are allowed. He goes for an interview.

"Name?"

"John Smith."

"Occupation?"

"Plumber."

"Religion?"

"Goy." '

Evelyn was dashing in and out from the kitchen, bringing food, taking away used plates; her daughters helped her but so did Chris. They had eggs in salt water and Evelyn's chicken soup with kneidlach (Ida, who until this point had remained silent, said, 'Nice. I like them doughy.')

Then the noise began. The adults chatted, crockery chimed, the kids laughed loudly and they also managed to digest Evelyn's roast chicken (she had jumped, for this special occasion, to recipe 74: with orange); there were potato latkes and bowls of (in Ida's opinion, raw) vegetables. Pudding was a selection of flour-free pastries: chocolate brownies, coconut macaroons and - Evelyn's speciality - kichlach.

Abby found the afikomen in the cupboard under the stairs and was given a box of sweets as a gift. The children chatted and laughed, David quiet although Ruth did see him smile a few times. She sent him looks of love with her eyes.

The singing began: 'Chad Gadya' with everyone assigned a role, be it cat, dog or goat whose noise they had to make; 'Echad Miyodea' and 'Adir Hu', finishing with 'Next year, in Jerusalem'. Morris sang with gusto, thumping the table for emphasis and then came his moment. He stood up. Evelyn hoped that his joke would be appropriate for the children to hear. He didn't always gauge it correctly.

'So…Moishe goes to the tailor's and sees a sign in the window. It says: (monotone voice) "What do you think? I make my suits for nothing."

Great, thinks Moishe. He goes in, chooses a suit and takes it away.

"What do you think you're doing?" asks the tailor chasing him outside.

"Look at your sign," says Moishe: "What do you think? I make my suits for nothing."

"No, no," says the tailor. "This is what it says: What do you think? I make my suits for

nothing!" '

Laughter all round (apart from Ida) and then came the conga (Ida abstained), the kids weaving in and out of the room, hands on the waist of the person in front, the mess, the noise, the chaos and the fun. It was great but Harold could feel himself overwhelmed. He stood at the kitchen door, breathing in the cool night air. Phew! He loved the mayhem. He loved the quiet! His chest felt a bit tight sometimes these days but he rubbed it with his hand, took some deep breaths and he felt okay.

Evelyn carried dirty dishes to the kitchen, others helping her, rolling up the tablecloths like giant snowballs, clearing everything away.

By the time everyone had left and Miriam and her family were in bed (she and Chris in the spare room, and Hannah and Daniel in what was her old bedroom) it was nearly 2 a m and everyone agreed - as they did every year – that it had been the best seder ever.

The following morning, Ruth rang her parents to thank them and asked to speak to Miriam.

'Hi Ruthie. What's up?'

'I've had an idea, Mims, and wanted your reaction.'

'Okay.' Miriam sat on the sofa and pushed the door shut against the family noise. 'Go on.'

'I've been worrying about David and his barmitzvah. As you know, it's coming up but I don't see him doing it alone. He's so shy, as you know and lacking in confidence. Also, he struggles with the Hebrew the way our girls haven't. He's now so anxious about it that I don't think he can manage it. I just wondered. He and Daniel get on so well together. Maybe they could do it jointly?'

'Does that ever happen?'

'Well, when there are twins, yes. Should I ask Rabbi Woolf about it?'

'Yes, I don't see why not. Before we ask the boys, you mean?'

Ruth noticed that she said 'ask' not 'tell' but she remained quiet on that. They needed to pull together, not apart.

'Yes, let me ask him first. If he says no, then that's that.'

Ruth sometimes wondered if Rabbi Woolf ever said no to anything. When she saw him, she always found him warm, open and amenable.

'So do boys ever have joint barmitzvahs?' she asked him, sitting in his crammed office.

'Yes, when there are twins. We even had triplets once. We give them the option.'

'Well, these are first cousins, as you know - David and Daniel - but they are both anxious about it and Miriam and I thought that it would help their confidence to do it together and they are only a few months apart in age.'

'Great,' said Rabbi Woolf, taking out the shul diary from his drawer. 'Let's look at some possible dates.'

11

Ruth

The problem with Mims is that she's made her choices, as have I, but then she's always wanted what I have as well. It happened all the time when we were children. We'd go to The Silver Diner, our favourite restaurant, with its red leather banquettes and desserts in a glass cabinet, look at the large, glossy menu and then Mum and Dad would let us choose. Let's say I wanted burger and fries and Mims chose steak and salad. Then when the waiter brought us our meal, Mims would regret her choice and look longingly at my plate until I let her have some of mine.

Another example: we shared a bedroom until we were seven and ten and then we had our own rooms. Mum said we could each choose a colour scheme for the wallpaper, curtains and bedding but that we'd then have to stick with our decision. She was always so fair but firm (she could be quite cross with us when we misbehaved) something I've tried to replicate with my own kids although I probably indulge them more than I should. I chose a pale lemon, being quite a cautious, understated person but Mims is wilder, more adventurous, more impulsive. She chose huge blue flowers with gold centres against a pink background. Of course, you can guess what happened. She loved the décor for the first month and then she grew sick of it and found it oppressive (it even gave her nightmares); so then she spent most of her time in my calm room, cramping my style.

This pattern continued into adulthood. After school I went to a kibbutz and then to Leeds to study Maths. I've always loved numbers. Accountancy suits me; it's precise, careful but also requires more courageous decisions than people realise. Mims went to India, changed her mind about her career several times, before eventually deciding to train as a teacher.

I knew that I'd only marry a Jewish man as I wanted to have a Jewish home, with the warmth of my parents' house but more observant. That's very important to me. There was no point dating a gentile man as I simply wouldn't marry him. I hope very much that my children marry within the faith. Why would I not want them to continue the traditions and heritage that I so value? That isn't the only reason I send them to a Jewish school. I also want them to be true to their identity and know as much as they can about Judaism so that they are well-informed.

Making a happy Jewish family home is everything to me. When you have children, you look at your own childhood and decide what you want to replicate, what to change. There are so many things that my parents got right, in my opinion: a strong family unit, many lovely occasions such as picnics and holidays, responsible, a decent life but also fun. What I would change is the religious aspect. My parents are socially, culturally Jewish but not regular shul attenders. Simon and I are much more involved. It's like a seesaw: my parents are (religiously) in the middle. Mims is at one end (more secular) and I am at the other (more observant).

Jews marrying non-Jews dilutes the faith. That's a fact. It is unlikely, then, that their children will lead a Jewish life and then the whole lineage disappears. The Orthodox will always exist, having many children who will continue their traditions; but other Jews, like us, want our strand of Judaism to survive, too. We have a duty to continue the line.

I don't agree with our Uncle Gerald who's turned his back on his roots. He would say it's his choice, of course, but I don't think you choose whether you are Jewish or not. I think it is a privilege that you are born into and you shouldn't take it for granted. I think it's wrong that Sebastian and Jo have no knowledge of Hebrew or the festivals or anything. They are totally ignorant. That's denying them their ancestry. I don't agree when people say that their children can choose whether to be Jewish or not, as Gerald's children have no choice at all. How can they opt for something they know nothing about? It's a bit like asking someone whether they would like to move to a country that they've never heard of.

Gerald's hard-line position means that we don't see him and his family very often and we don't know his kids, our cousins. It's broken up the family rather.

I don't mind who Mims chose to marry. Chris is a lovely man but I don't like the way that she blames others for her decisions. It's not my fault that they decided to live in a non-Jewish area and can't find a challah each week, but she makes me feel bad about it. We're back to the menu and decorating choices.

She made an enormous fuss about Daniel's bris. It's part of our culture and the baby doesn't suffer for more than two minutes. Because there was no mohel in their area, they had to drive to London and I helped her arrange it. I've done an enormous amount for her over the years. She asks me to send her things that she can't get – Judaica, cards, candles – and I don't mind but I do think that sometimes she forgets how busy I am. I also don't really like that view of Judaism – that you can buy it online or get it sent to you. It is a way of life, a deep commitment, not something you dip in and out of.

I'm not saying that she hasn't been there for me. I love Mims. When I had my two miscarriages she dropped everything and rushed down to London to sit with me in the hospital and we wept together. I think I've been a good sister to her, too. When she left school she went a bit wild with boys and there may have been some dabbling in drugs (we kept it from our parents); I tried to help her to become more mature and sensible. At one stage, she thought that she was pregnant (luckily just a false alarm) but I went to the doctor with her.

I sometimes think that she is jealous of me and my life but I am also sometimes jealous of her. She is a free spirit: her long, curly hair, her glowing skin, her eyes which always seem bright and alive.

Meeting Simon was a bit of luck. He's calm and doesn't get sucked into my crazy family when they're all talking at the same time. His parents live in Israel now with Joel, his brother, who has severe special needs, so inevitably all the chagim are at my parents' home and he's really good with them, tolerant and kind, but he also keeps slightly distant which is good. He doesn't get drawn into the dramas but hangs back, which I appreciate. At those manic times, we need someone solid.

Mims thinks that everyone else's life is easier than hers but we've had plenty to deal with, too: my miscarriages, Simon's business going through some very difficult times and our worries over David.

Friends tell me that boys are easier to raise but that hasn't been my experience. Our girls, Leah and Abby, are sunny-natured and have both been easy-going, compliant. But David is different. Maybe it was hard for him being sandwiched between two cheery, easy going girls but he's always struggled. I lie in bed, sometimes, worrying about his future. Will he marry? What job will he be able to hold down? Will he find life too hard to cope with?

It started young. The Jewish school, Hillel, has a nursery attached to it and all our children have gone there. His lovely teacher, Miss Simon, called us in tell us that David wasn't mixing with the other kids, that he was bit of a loner. He lacked confidence.

It was a blow for Simon and me. We are quite quiet people and thought that his personality was the same as ours, a bit shy; but she felt that she it was more worrying than that. He also struggled academically.

These issues have continued throughout his life so far. We've tried to support him in every way we can and just want him be happy but he is still timid and anxious. I knew that, for him, a barmitzvah would be a huge ordeal. So now that Mims and I have agreed (and of course, the rabbi was supportive, as ever) that he and Daniel will do one together, that's a relief. They're close in age and get on really well. It will still be stressful, though: we're all so different. We'll just have to see how it goes.

Mims gives mixed messages. On the one hand, she's happy for me to send her things that she needs and can't get; but then, if I overstep the line in her eyes, she thinks that I'm controlling. You can't win with her.

At times, I've found life very hard. I've always worked full-time and what with three children and the house to run, it's a lot. I worry about Simon's business (we have a big mortgage on the house), the kids, life!

I don't like it when Mims and I fall out or get stressed with each other. But we always make peace on shabbat and call each other. That is sacred. Nothing interferes with that. Those moments are precious.

Recipe: Israel's horseradish

Grow the plant in your garden.

Just before Pesach, pick, peel and slice.

Watch as everyone's eyes water.

Recipe: charoshet

Take some nuts, raisins, walnuts and dates.

Drown them in kiddush wine.

Mix together into a paste.

Don't worry if it is sticky and heavy. It's supposed to symbolise the mortar used for building the pyramids.

If you have any left over, use it for cementing a wall.

12

Brachot in Bordeaux

After Pesach but before Ramadan, Miriam and Mehreen could identify eight free days. The two families had been away before, just camping in the UK, and they'd all got on so well (in spite of sporadic rain and over-familiar cows). This time they decided to go to France: it was the Easter holidays so no school. Ruth and her family had gone to Israel to see Simon's parents and brother. Harold and Evelyn would enjoy the peace and quiet, especially as Harold hadn't been feeling so well of late. (He'd wondered if it was due to Evelyn's raw chicken but surely he'd built up immunity to that by now?)

Fields of sunflowers lifted their golden faces to the light. Vineyards stretched as far as the sky and each village was more delightful than its predecessor: red rooves; windy, cobbled streets; markets where home-grown vegetables, still mud-encrusted, were sold in wicker baskets beneath red-striped awnings.

Along they meandered through the Charente in their hired van, the kids singing songs with many verses, the adults chatting and taking it in turns to drive. They stopped on the way to have a picnic: baguettes and cheese, tomatoes plump and juicy in a brown paper bag; peaches large and white-fleshed.

Their gîte was as beautiful as the online photo had promised: duck egg blue shutters flung open to the sun; red geraniums frothing from terracotta pots; stone and flint walls - and a pool!

While the adults unpacked, the kids were already changed and in the water. Whoops of laughter and sounds of splashes filled the French air.

And that was how the holiday continued: enjoyment and fun. There were meals eaten on the terrace (they always ate vegetarian food when they were together). Chris and Afzal did most of the cooking: there was a barbecue for them to use and a table and chairs to seat everyone; and when they could coax the kids out of the pool, they went on day trips. Bordeaux was beautiful, Angoulême delightful with its hilly streets and quaint shops, and there were long, lazy days spent by the river, dangling their feet in its cool, dappled waters, marbled by the sun.

Miriam felt herself relax. She worried less about school, about her Judaism, about her kids and the happier she was, so were they. She slept better and felt closer to Chris than ever. They made love in the wrought iron bed, conscious of its creaking.

At first, they all moved around together as a tribe but, as Miriam felt more confident that the area was safe, she let the kids go out on their own, in pairs or as a group, or to stay at the gite while the adults went out on their own. They had her mobile number in case of emergencies even though the signal was rather precarious.

One day the two couples went to Riberac market where there were home-made baskets, cheese stalls and beautiful antique furniture. Miriam and Mehreen drooled over a gold-edged mirror, two candlesticks bent in elegant curls at the front. They even thought about taking it back home until they realised that was unrealistic. So they contented themselves with a basket each, Miriam's with flowers, Mehreen's with butterflies, embroidered on the front, which they swung as they strolled: reminders of a wonderful holiday.

Miriam thought: there is no other family with whom we get on so well. The men were friends, the women very close, the kids also and it just worked; whereas with Ruth, Chris and Simon had little in common apart from being married to sisters and, with some of Chris's academic colleagues,

Miriam didn't really connect with the wives. Religion wasn't mentioned much on the holiday (it was good to be somewhere where it wasn't a consideration) but one evening, Mehreen spoke to them about being Muslim in the UK and how, when there were terrible extremist incidents such as bombings or suicides, she feared for her children at school the next day and what negative reactions they might receive. Most Muslims, she told them, were moderate and law-abiding, just wanting from life what everyone wanted: peace, good health, a steady career, a happy family life.

And when it was shabbat, Miriam took out her candles, a challah (specially saved in the freezer for this holiday) and wine carefully stowed in a bag and they did the brachot and Mehreen and her family watched with interest and respect. Miriam rang her sister in Israel and they wished each other 'gut shabbos' as they always did.

It was the penultimate day of the holiday. It had been a great success and the couples had decided that they would do this again in the future. For the last time, the adults had gone out on their own, for coffee and to buy some take-home treats from the boulangerie including macaroons for Evelyn.

As soon as they entered the gîte, Daniel and Jamil came running out.

'It's Aunty Ruth on the landline,' said David, agitated. 'She's left three messages. She couldn't get through to your mobile. You need to ring her.'

Miriam dropped her basket and the cheeses and macaroons tumbled onto the stone floor. 'Why? What's happened?'

'I don't know, Mum. She wouldn't say.'

Miriam ran to the phone and rang her sister in Israel. Chris and the others went to the pool, realising that she needed space.

'Ruthie, what is it?'

'Are you sitting down, Mims?'

Miriam collapsed onto a chair, her heart racing. 'Now I am.'

'It's Dad. He's had a heart attack.'

'Oh no.' Miriam felt tears spring to her eyes. Her wonderful father. 'Is he alright?'

'He's stable. In hospital and being well cared for. I didn't know if I should ring you or not.'

'Of course you did the right thing. Poor Daddy. Is Mum okay?'

'Yeah. Be strong. We're trying to get earlier flights back to the UK. I'll let you know when I know more. Love you.'

'Love you Ruthie.'

'Love you, Mims.'

Miriam wept, the weave of the chair hard beneath her cotton dress. The tears came uncontrollably: her lovely dad, who was always there: kind, patient, wry. There was something about his stocky build that was comforting, as if he would always be there, never waver.

When Miriam calmed down, she decided to tell the family. Chris and Afzal were on the terrace, Jamil and Daniel leaping off lilos in the pool.

'Everyone,' said Miriam, 'I have some bad news, I'm afraid.' Chris looked concerned.

Then she realised that they weren't all there. 'Where are Hannah and Taj?' She saw a glance pass between Daniel and Jamil and then she realised.

Climbing the stairs of the gite to Hannah's room (she'd been allotted her own, being the only girl whereas the three boys had to share) Miriam's heart was beating fast, her thoughts tumbling through her head. Her poor daddy…luckily the holiday was nearly over….they'd drive to see him from Heathrow. She stood outside Hannah's shut door and listened. She could hear laughter, noises of pleasure, loving sounds.

It confirmed what she'd already suspected.

Hannah and Taj had known each other for years, ever since Miriam had taken the job at Mounthill, become close to Mehreen and introduced the families to each other. The kids had always been friends but it was only here on holiday that she'd noticed a tenderness developing between Hannah and Taj. There were subtle signs: when they went kayaking down the river one day, Taj held his hand out for Hannah as she left the boat and when she took it, she blushed. When they were at a restaurant one night, all eight of them sitting beneath a clambering vine bearing grapes like glass marbles, Miriam noticed Taj and Hannah feeding each other chips. And then, in the pool, they were swimming near each other all the time, splashing and messing around. One day, Taj (who was always quite spirited) flipped Hannah off the lilo and then caught her in his arms, laughing.

She'd even mentioned these observations to Chris in bed. 'I think there's something going on between Hannah and Taj.'

'Your imagination,' he laughed and stroked her dark hair.

Miriam summoned up all her courage and knocked on the door. She could just imagine them springing apart at the sound, and tidying themselves up.

The door opened. Hannah looked flushed and Miriam noticed that the buttons on her shirt were done up incorrectly, as if in a hurry, so that the shirt hung lopsidedly. Taj was standing behind her, looking uncomfortable.

'Sorry,' said Miriam, 'but there's been some bad news about grandad. Can you come downstairs, please?'

Minutes later, they were all sitting on the terrace while Miriam stood up and spoke. It reminded her of briefing pupils about rules before a theatre trip.

'I'm so sorry to have to tell you all, but Daniel and Hannah's grandad Harold – my dad - has had a heart attack.'

There were gasps all round and Miriam could see that there were tears glassing Hannah's eyes.

'He's alright,' Miriam added. 'He's in hospital and is stable.'

Hannah wiped her eyes. 'Can we see him?'

Miriam noticed that Hannah tended to articulate her feelings whereas Daniel tended to keep his locked within.

'Yes, sweetheart. We'll go straight from the airport.'

The atmosphere of the holiday changed. The combination of the discovery of Hannah and Taj, coupled with the news about Harold, had dampened the mood. The joy, the spontaneity and laughter, dissipated in the air like steam.

Chris and Afzal prepared lunch – pitta bread, dips and salads – and they ate together on the terrace, beneath the striped parasol as they'd done before but they were all subdued. It was quiet. Hardly any conversation.

They packed the next day, the gîte cleaned, the beds stripped and the linens rolled into cotton icebergs. It was such a shame that what had been a wonderful holiday had ended sourly, like a delicious meal followed by bitter coffee. Miriam wanted to speak to Mehreen about Hannah and Taj but there was no time.

At Heathrow, they all parted with hugs and embraces, Hannah and Taj hanging on longer than the others, and then they made their separate ways: Mehreen and family back to the Midlands, Miriam and family to the hospital.

As the families went their own ways, Taj and Hannah turned round to blow each other a kiss.

13

Simon

From the outside, I'm sure that people see us as the perfect family: lovely house, both sets of parents happily married, great kids, good business, no real worries about money.

But if I've learned one thing about life, it's not to judge people or situations from the outside. As Rabbi Hillel said, we don't know how it feels to be someone else until we walk in their shoes.

I see it at the tennis club in Goldwell Hill that Ruth and I belong to and enjoy: like-minded people connected by a sport we love. When you first meet a couple (and we like playing in pairs) they seem straightforward to you, their lives fine; but once you get to know them, they reveal their issues, their struggles. As they learn to trust you, they confide in you and then you find it out: the first marriage that faltered, the bereavement, the loss, the business collapse.

It's like the thrillers and spy novels that I like to read, with heroes more adventurous and dynamic than me. They're just names at the start and then you get to know them, like peeling the layers of an onion. I'm the opposite to the life and soul of the party. I'm the quiet one, with a drink in his hand, looking for Ruth.

I suppose it goes back to childhood. Joel, two years younger than me, has always needed a lot of help. He can't speak, is incontinent, wheelchair-bound, and needs constant vigilance. He's very limited although he knows me as he always breaks into a grin when I enter. I ruffle his hair or tickle his tummy. He likes that.

The doctors say that he was deprived of oxygen at birth and my parents adore him. They could easily afford to put him in a home but they won't. My mother gave up her job as a solicitor and looked after Joel while Dad ran the business. They made aliyah after I graduated and love living near our cousins in Israel, where they feel supported.

No-one's to blame but I think my childhood was very affected by this situation. Understandably, the attention had to be on Joel so I learned to be quiet, self-contained, to amuse myself. I read adventure stories, went to other people's houses (it was difficult having friends round) and I immersed myself in sport: football, tennis and cricket.

My parents wanted me to look after myself but also to excel and I found that duality hard. I had to succeed but without the attention, praise and coaxing that I needed. I've never been very confident and it was hard at times, lonely. When Dad asked me to join the business, after my degree in Economics from Leeds, I agreed to please him. It wasn't really what I wanted to do although I know I'm lucky to have that opportunity.

When they went to Israel, he passed it to me and I now own it. Mum and Dad get a stipend and we have set up a trust fund so that Joel will be looked after for life. With Ruth beside me, overseeing the accounts, it's great.

Finding Ruth was life-changing. We met at the Leeds Student Jewish Society where there were talks, services and meals organised. I hadn't had much experience with women until then and I have always thought myself plain-looking, but I can honestly say that as soon as I met Ruth I knew we would get married. I've never regretted it.

She's beautiful, confident, fun and we have so much in common. I feel that I am the luckiest man on the planet to have married her. We are a strong team. Our shared Judaism, our values and our desire to raise our children in a loving Jewish family is very important to us. I'd be distraught if my kids married out. If you value your heritage, why would you not want it to continue?

I don't understand people who say they are proud of their Judaism but who then marry non-Jews. Why do that?

Our girls are like their mother: bright, assertive, confident but I worry about David. His issues are very different from Joel's but it does feel as if history's repeating itself. We find ourselves focusing on him more than on Leah and Abby.

If we want to go on holiday, for example, the first thoughts are: what about David? If there's only a communal pool, he might find that daunting. He doesn't like being squashed into planes or trains for too long. He isn't keen on loud noises and he isn't easy about food. He doesn't always sleep well.

When I was growing up, if someone invited us somewhere, my parents' first thought was always: how will it be for Joel? Never: how will it be for Simon? And now I find that Ruth and I do the same. How will it be for David? Not Leah or Abby.

We've had him tested and, at one stage, the teacher at the private Jewish school, Hillel, which all our kids have attended and loved, thought that he might be on the autistic spectrum, but apparently not. He does have special needs and so we've had to pay for a learning support teacher to help him and he's just very shy and fragile.

When Ruth suggested the double barmitzvah with his cousin Daniel, I wasn't at all sure about it. I like Chris and Miriam but we're very different people and also, Ruth and Miriam have a real sisterly love-hate relationship. That sibling rivalry is alien to me as Joel and I never had that. He came first and I just had to accept it.

When Ruth and Miriam clash, I hate it: it's unpleasant and Ruth gets so upset. Of course, I take Ruth's side and Chris takes Miriam's and it feels like two tribes at war, so much uglier than when we play tennis doubles. That is friendly competition, but this sisterly thing is another issue altogether. We all suffer (Harold and Evelyn too) and are hurt and raw, but then, blow me down, Ruth and Miriam make up and carry on as if nothing happened. It can leave us feeling bruised and confused.

Morris is good fun although he can rather overdo the jokes at times and they aren't always appropriate with children around. I don't really know Ruth's Uncle Gerald as he won't join in with simchas. It seem strange to us that he's rejected his roots but everyone has to make their own choices. We occasionally meet them for picnics and meals but if there's any hint of any Jewish element, they won't come. It's odd. I don't understand it.

Harold and Evelyn, however, are lovely people: warm, friendly, always welcoming. She's a terrible cook and Ruth and I have often worried about getting food poisoning, but it's never happened. Harold's delightful and kind. He's sometimes asked me for business advice and I've had to tread very carefully. He's very old-fashioned and not really suited for this cut-throat world at all. So I proceed with caution, trying to advise him but always being very careful about what I say. I wouldn't want him to think that I'm being patronising.

But caution comes easily to me. I am with Harold as I always am: careful, conscious of how I come across, holding myself back.

Recipe: chopped liver

Fry some liver and onion.

Mix it in the machine. Why do it by hand?

Hard-boil an egg, shell and crumble over the liver.

The end result should look like a burial mound covered in crushed chrysanthemums.

14

Harold's Hospital Herrings

Hospital had some advantages for Harold. It was peaceful! No family tsores!

He lay quietly in his bed in a ward with only three other men. They were pleasant enough, reserved, no-one in the mood for any conversation. One frail man read books about the SAS which seemed bizarre, a million miles away from his unfortunate physical state. Clean white sheets bound Harold in his narrow bed, where he passed the time reading murder mysteries, doing crosswords and keeping in touch with family through phone calls and texts.

However, the food! It was insipid and bland and that was on a good day.

So he tried the kosher menu, not that he and Evelyn kept strictly kosher at home but it was worth a try. It was better than the main menu but it still tasted mass-produced, not home-made, not flavoursome. Objectively, he knew that Evelyn wasn't the best cook in the world but he'd become used to her food, her undercooked chicken and her sloping cakes, all created with tenderness and love. He remembered with relish Shlossy's borsht and Rivka's pastries and he salivated at the thought of it all.

The heart attack itself had come as quite a shock. For weeks, months maybe, he'd sometimes felt a tightening in his chest which gripped him like a vice, shooting also down his arm, but then released again. He always ignored both it and Evelyn's telling him to see a doctor.

'Doctor, shmoctor, what do I need one for?'

And then one evening (they were at home luckily) he'd felt particularly stressed. He was worrying about work: the factory really wasn't doing that well any more. The clients they'd always served were now downsizing, going into old age homes or, sadly, dying: in all three cases, going to a place where sideboards, dressing tables and bedside cabinets weren't required. He knew their stuff was old-fashioned and that youngsters now wanted shiny, inexpensive, white Swedish furniture and who could blame them? Simon, his son-in-law, had tried to advise him but it was all too modern and technological for him: online this, online that. Profits and sales were down. It was coming to an end. Sadly, Harold had to sack a few loyal employees and that nearly broke his heart – or certainly put a strain on it.

Then, standing at the garden door one evening after another of Evelyn's hefty meals, the latkes dropping through his body to his feet, the grip came again around his heart, then down his arm and he fell to the floor. The next he knew he was in an ambulance with Evelyn looking down at him, crying.

He'd been in hospital for five days now and had been told off by several doctors who, in different ways, all gave the same message: Harold was overworked and overweight.

He wasn't so keen on that prefix 'over'. He wished they'd say 'under'.

He was only allowed two visitors at a time, between 6 and 8 in the evening, so it was usually Ruth and Evelyn who came, bringing him fresh fruit (so many grapes, he could start his own vineyard) and wordsearches.

So he was thrilled one evening when Miriam and Hannah came in to see him (all arranged through Evelyn).

'What a lovely surprise. I thought you were still on holiday.'

‘We’ve come straight from the airport,’ said Hannah, holding her zaider’s hand.

‘How are you, Dad? asked Miriam, holding the other.

‘Much better for seeing you lovelies,’ said Harold, smiling.

And they spoke to him and chatted and joked but all the time Miriam could see that he wasn’t really that well. His face looked puffy and pasty, bags under his eyes, and the heart monitor he was attached to beeped and hummed, making him look vulnerable.

After twenty minutes, Miriam and Hannah left the ward and let Chris and Daniel have a chance to see Harold.

So it was in the hospital so-called ‘family room’ that Miriam and Hannah spoke.

‘Hannah, sweetie,’ she said tentatively, ‘I don’t want to intrude but is there something going on between you and Taj?’

Hannah blushed slightly and tucked her hair behind one ear, which she did when cornered. ‘Oh you noticed?’

‘Yes, on holiday.’

‘It’s been a few months now. It just sort of happened naturally, when we were out with friends. We didn’t plan it that way.’

‘No, I understand.’

‘It isn’t a problem, is it? Because you and Mehreen are friends. Or the Jewish thing?’

Miriam paused for a moment. Was it a problem? Ruth and Evelyn would think so. But did she? It made life more complicated but then she'd married a non-Jew so who was she to comment? Anyway, who was talking about marriage? They were seventeen.

She took Hannah's hand in hers.

'No, of course it isn't, sweetheart. Just be sensible, please.'

Hannah rolled her eyes. 'We will, Mum. We're not children. Seriously.'

Chris and Daniel didn't stay long. Harold asked for Miriam to be brought in again.

'Yes, Dad,' she said, 'what is it?'

'The food here's lousy. I miss your mum's terrible cooking and the excitement of whether you're going to get poisoning or not. Bring me some chopped herring. Your mother and Ruth won't agree to it.'

'But Dad -'

'Do it for me, Miriam.'

Miriam sighed and smiled. 'Okay. I'll see what I can do.'

The following morning, before returning to the Midlands, Miriam popped into a deli and got Harold his favourite pickled food - cucumbers, herrings, cabbage - and smuggled them in, concealed in a white plastic bag.

'You're an angel,' he said, opening the bag and sniffing its contents, like a pickle junkie.

The following evening, Morris and Ida went in as the designated pair. Morris bemoaned the fact that he was always lumped with the nudnik, like (reluctant) conjoined twins. It was like the funny man and his sidekick, the straight woman.

So they entered the ward: Morris, large, bearded, imposing, and Ida, sour, small: the elephant and the mouse.

Harold was sitting up in bed, propped by pillows. The windows had been opened and the air con on high at the request of the other patients: the smell of pickles was overwhelming.

'Harold,' greeted Morris as they arrived. He sat on one side of the bed and Ida, scowling, sat on the other. Somehow they seemed to symbolise his life: joy and pain, delight and sorrow. It reminded Harold of a sermon that Rabbi Woolf had given on Yom Kippur some years back. He quoted Rabbi Simcha Bunim, a great Polish Hasid who said that everyone must have two pockets, with a note in each one, so that he or she can reach into one or the other, depending on the need. When depressed, one should reach into the right pocket, and, there, find the words, 'The world was created for me.' But when feeling too self-satisfied, one should find in the other pocket the message, 'I am but dust and ashes.'

Here was Morris to lift him up and Ida to bring him down so that Harold felt he was a pivot in the centre of a seesaw, hovering between hope and despair. The saint and the sinner. The angel and the devil.

'How are you feeling?' asked Morris. It was sad to see his lovely brother-in-law wired up to a machine.

'Well,' Harold wobbled his hand to gesture so-so, cacha-cacha.

'So….' Morris led himself in. 'Moishe goes to see the matchmaker. She says, "Don't leave it too late, Moishe. I have just the girl you need." "Don't bother," says Moishe. "At home I have two sisters who look after all my needs." "Family isn't the same as a wife," said the matchmaker. "I said two sisters," said Moishe. "I didn't say they were mine." '

The cardiology machine's previously straight line went zigzag as Harold chuckled.

'Don't make me laugh,' he said. 'The doctor said no excitement.'

'How's the food?' asked Ida. 'Undercooked?'

That brought Harold back down to earth. 'No,' he said, 'the opposite. It's such a purée you could feed it to a baby.'

The heart monitor levelled to a neutral line.

The Steel family's drive home was in stark contrast to that they'd done in the other direction, only nine days earlier. Going to the airport, they'd been excited, full of anticipation, singing songs all in fake French accents. 'Ten green bottles, 'anging on ze wall.' Now, the atmosphere was more subdued. Hannah was missing Taj with a physical pain and texting him back and forth. Daniel was worrying about his barmitzvah and the portion he had to learn. Chris was thinking about his book, and wondering how best to link the details of Shakespeare's life and especially the loss of Hamnet with the depiction of lost children in his plays. Was there a danger in making too simplistic links? Hannah was thinking about her dad. And they were all fully aware that the following day it was back to school/work.

Only at lunch on Tuesday did Miriam get the chance to catch up with Mehreen.

They chose their salads and sat opposite each other in the canteen.

'Thank you again for a great holiday,' said Miriam, tentatively.

'It was amazing,' said Mehreen.

Miriam paused, choosing her words carefully. 'Did you guess about Hannah and Taj?'

Mehreen put down her cutlery, giving the subject her full attention. 'I had a suspicion and then, on holiday, it became obvious. We're so fond of Hannah -'

'- as we are of Taj. He's a wonderful young man.'

'However...'

'I know. The families won't like it. What do we do?'

'I think if we oppose it, they'll dig their heels in so let's go along with it and see what happens.'

'I agree, Mehreen. We always agree.'

Harold was allowed out of hospital after ten days but with strict instructions: he had to rest and watch his weight. It seemed to him that these two commands contradicted each other. How could he exercise and also rest but one decision he'd made, he discussed with Evelyn.

'I've been thinking,' he said. They'd just finished a meal consisting of Evelyn's undercooked chicken and enough greenery to feed a rabbit for a year (her attempt to help him eat healthily). Harold munched it obediently: he'd raid the fridge later when Evelyn had gone to bed. 'I think it's time to sell the business.'

'I agree, darling,' said his wife. 'I'm so pleased to hear you say that.'

'I feel bad about the staff but it's time to take it easier. Will you carry on teaching?'

'For a few more years, I think. What will you do in your retirement?'

He reached for her hand. 'I don't know. Take a Swedish lover. Run a pig farm. Learn Italian.'

Evelyn laughed. 'Or you could tackle the DIY jobs that I've been asking you to do for ten years.'

'Yeah, yeah,' said Harold and they kissed. 'I'd rather have a Swedish lover.'

The factory was sold. It took a while and the price offered was disappointing but Harold was relieved. He could pay off their mortgage and put aside the rest in savings for their pension.

On his last day at the factory Harold gathered together his staff. There were tears on many faces. He looked around at the African, Asian and Greek staff for whom he had a great affection.

'I thank you all from the bottom of my heart attack' - everyone laughed - 'for all that you've done for this business. Today's a sad day as I leave the factory started by my grandfather Isaac and then passed on to my father Abie and then to me. I'm so pleased that the new owners have kept you all on and I wish every one of you all the very best.'

Applause erupted and Harold wept.

Driving home, the contents of his office in two cardboard boxes, Harold concluded that he'd spent his life in the wrong job. He should have been a rabbi or a teacher. He wasn't cut-throat or ambitious enough for business. He wondered how many others had been in the wrong job, marriage or home and how lucky he was in two of those three areas, at least.

So he started the next phase of his life, experiencing a mixture of failure and relief.

15

Leah

When you have a brother with special needs, like David, the light of the family does shine more on him. If we want to have a meal out, we need to choose a quiet calm place, not too much mayhem or chaos, because of David. Noise bothers him. If we go on holiday, likewise. Disneyworld: too busy and mad. A rural location's better. If we even want to watch a film together, it has to be something David likes, which usually means sci-fi or *Star Trek*, whereas Abby and me like Disney and rom-coms.

I'm not blaming anyone for this. It's just the situation. Mum and Dad are great and Abby and I are very close, even though we're ten years apart. I'm sure we'll always get on, even when we're married and have our own children. I love David too but he can't be very loving back. He isn't able to be.

Having a brother like him makes you more aware of other people's sufferings and makes you more compassionate. When we go out and I see families with disabled children, I feel great sympathy for them because I know that their lives will be tough. I would like to do something caring one day, maybe be a psychologist or work with children, as I've seen it from the inside. It wouldn't just be theory with me.

Of course, my dad has a brother with special needs and a son (albeit very different) so it makes him quiet and thoughtful. He doesn't speak a lot about it. He just gets on with life but sometimes he looks serious and I wonder what he's thinking.

I think I'm one of the luckiest people I know, as I am surrounded by love: my parents and siblings; grandparents and aunts and uncles on both sides; my school Hillel where we have all gone from nursery to sixth form; Goldwell Hill Shul where we have been all our lives and know everyone. Also, we have a beautiful big house with a lovely garden and we have our own bedrooms. Some people might think that I'm a bit spoilt as I do have the clothes, books and toys I want but I appreciate them and am grateful. Judaism puts a lot of emphasis on tzedakah, charity, and we have all given our own pocket money to good causes. Mum and Dad insist on that.

Although I love singing and dancing and messing around, I also think seriously about issues such as the environment and politics. I hope one day to marry someone Jewish and to have a family, not unlike my own. I wouldn't change much about the way my parents have brought me up. Maybe they could be a bit more jolly and not so serious (celebrate and laugh more) but I suppose they have a lot on their minds, what with their jobs, which are heavy, and with David.

I'm starting to go out more with friends and Mum and Dad can be a bit funny about that. Fridays are spent at home and we aren't allowed out. When I do go out, Mum wants to know where I am and I have to text and say that I am safe. Dad keeps quiet but Mum says what she feels. She comments on my clothes sometimes and doesn't like me wearing too much make-up. But I'm young. Life is meant to be fun, not just hard work.

Most kids criticise their parents but mine are pretty good.

I just hope they let me have the freedom to make my own choices – and mistakes.

Recipe: chopped herring

Get some herring.

Chop it.

Fumigate the house.

16

Shalom Aleichem / Saalam Alaikum

The idea for the joint family meal came, as did many of their ideas, from the canteen lunch that Miriam and Mehreen shared.

'They do seem very fond of each other,' said Mehreen, finishing her yoghurt.

'They do. It's sweet but we're both in the same situation as far as family goes. It's not going to go down well.'

'No. I agree. It's not.'

'Will you all come for a meal and we can discuss it then?' They cleared their trays away.

'We'd love to. Thank you. A new spin on meeting the parents.'

They chose a shabbat as Mehreen and her family had responded well to it in France; so Miriam's Hunt the Challah jaunt started again, but this time without success. Chris then surprised her by baking one. It was a little misshapen but was, without doubt, a golden challah.

'How did you know how to make it?' she asked, coming home after a long day at school, which had included a staff meeting and a parents' evening, and relishing the eggy smell.

'I looked online and there was a film on You Tube called 'How to make your own challah' and so I followed the instructions on how to plait it.'

Miriam hugged him. 'Thank you sweetheart.'

She laid the table with a white cloth and Chris helped her to prepare Jewish/Israeli food: fried fish and salads: chatzilim, egg salad, pitta bread and humus, roast beetroot, falafel and an array of pastries and sweets: halva, cinnamon cake and apple strudel. She and Mehreen had agreed that the meal would reflect both their traditions.

Mehreen brought food that she and Afzal had made: a plate of mahsi (aubergines, courgettes and vine leaves filled with rice), berber bread, a delicious lentil soup and an eggplant and onion stew.

With the table covered in lovely dishes and the eight of them seated at the table (Daniel and Jamil had to sit on garden chairs) Miriam lit the candles and sang the brachot on them, the wine and Chris's wonky challah; everyone said Amen.

Then Mehreen and her family said their blessing: Bless the food You have provided for us and save us from the punishment of the hellfire. *Bismillahi wa 'ala baraka-tillah.* In the name of God and with God's blessing.

They shared the food and ate. Miriam had a feeling of joy: here they were all together, with family and friends, sharing a beautiful meal. Hannah and Taj beamed side by side, the boys enjoyed being together and the couples always got on.

But after the meal, when the boys went to play, the adults were left with Hannah and Taj so, over coffee and pastries (Mehreen had baked baklava and basbousa, topped with nuts) Miriam chose her words carefully and broached the subject. Hannah could flare up at times and Miriam knew that she was pre-menstrual, so more touchy than usual. Her neck was already red, as if in defence.

'We're all very happy that you two are so in love,' she said. Taj and Hannah sat side by side.. 'But we want to have an honest conversation with you about when to tell the wider family. You have to understand that there may be some disapproval from them.'

'That's not our fault if they're racist,' said Hannah, her cheeks reddening. Taj took her hand to soothe her, his tendency to be more considered, less volatile.

'I know, darling, but older people have different ideas.'

'So that's their problem, not ours.' Hannah's indignation was almost palpable. Taj sat quietly beside her, a thoughtful young man.

'You're right, Hannah.' Miriam tried not to patronise her, to say, you don't understand what lies ahead. 'So when would you like the family to know about your relationship?'

'Maybe Danny's barmitzvah?' said Hannah.

'Good idea,' said Miriam, thinking as she agreed, that it wasn't.

'And we have a family gathering soon,' said Mehreen, 'so maybe Hannah would come along to that and we could do the introductions?'

Hannah and Taj seemed happy with that although neither could quite understand what all the fuss was about.

As Hannah said to her mum one evening, 'What's the big deal? Look at *Romeo and Juliet*. Look at Maria and Tony in *West Side Story*.'

Miriam smiled but thought that Hannah demonstrated her naivety in moments like these: both those tales ended with death and destruction and surely only showed how hard it was to make mixed marriages work. They were not the ideal examples that Hannah thought they were: quite the opposite.

Instead of this situation dividing Miriam and Mehreen, if anything it brought them even closer, as they understood each other's feelings. They each liked the other's child: there was no problem there but they were all too aware of the potential problems and family disapproval. Miriam would lie awake worrying: what if Hannah and Taj ending up marrying? What would the wedding ceremony be like? What religion would their children be? As Judaism is matrilineal and Islam patrilineal, each family would surely want their religion to prevail? (This seemed to Miriam something to celebrate, as the child could have both heritages, but she knew that not everyone would agree.) Then, in the morning, Miriam would wake in a cold sweat and think herself silly for worrying: they were only seventeen. It may not last. It may just fizzle out.

One day in the school canteen, Miriam and Mehreen sat together and the latter reported on her weekend.

'Well, we had the celebrations at my sister's house and I told them about Hannah and Taj. Nothing against her but there were some raised eyebrows and later my mother rang and raised her concerns with me. What about our heritage? Our traditions? They're being forgotten. She was disappointed.'

'Oh dear, Mehreen. I'm sorry,' said Miriam, feeling for her friend, feeling for herself. 'Maybe in time they'll come to accept it?'

But even as she tried to comfort Mehreen, she failed to convince herself.

Everything else was going well. Daniel was making good progress with learning his portion. Chris had turned a corner with his book and the publishers were pleased with it. School was fine. Everyone, including the problematic class she had, was more settled now. Even Lucas was handing in some of his work and occasionally answering the question set. Her dad was watching his weight and doing some exercise (although he still raided the biscuit tin when Evelyn was in bed). The main issue was the worry about Hannah and Taj.

A few times, Miriam had tried to broach the subject with Hannah but she could almost see the defensive barrier come down. Hannah had various stock answers:

'Taj and I love each other,' or 'No-one cares about those divisions any more,' or 'You hardly married the rabbi's son, did you, Mum?' and Miriam had no impressive answers to any of these.

Miriam could hardly say: 'marry a Jew' when she hadn't. It would be like chain-smoking parents telling their children not to start.

Looking back on her life, Miriam wondered to what extent parents should tell their children what to do. When she'd told her mum about Chris, she could smell the disappointment in the air but her mother had never intervened or tried to control her. Her father never commented on any decision at all. Was that right? If they'd said: 'marry a gentile and we'll disown you', would that have worked or would she have still chosen Chris over them? She loved him but could she have found a Jewish man to marry whom she loved as much?

The only person who'd intervened was Ida.

It was after another one of their famous shabbats when they were all together. Evelyn had cooked one of her staples (recipe 43: chicken and prunes) and everyone had added a secret bracha in their heads: Lord, please may I not get salmonella.

Morris had told another of his jokes over pudding:

'So...Esther's son Wolfie is dragged out to sea by a tidal wave. She wails at the edge of the beach.

“Wolfie! Wolfie, my son will be drowned.”

The lifeguard jumps into the raging waters, swims out and rescues Wolfie.

“Oh thank God,” she says, clutching her bewildered son. “But he had a hat.” ’

Coffee had been sipped; Leah had fallen asleep and was on the sofa, covered with a blanket; Ruth was helping Evelyn tidy away; Harold and Simon were having a chat about business; Morris and Chris talking about books (they always seemed to get on well, both being outsiders) and Ida and Miriam were left together in the dining room. It felt at the time like an accident but, in hindsight, it was probably engineered by the aunt. They gathered up all the unused cutlery, rolled the linen napkins and tablecloth into a ball, leaving the lit candles (Evelyn didn’t like them being blown out before their natural time), the kiddush cup and challah, sitting plump on its board like a mother duck on her nest.

‘So I see that you’re going out with a non-Jew,’ said Ida, sourly. She didn’t believe in gently tiptoeing into a subject. If she’d been a performer, there’d be no warm-up.

Miriam clutched the linen ball defensively to her chest. ‘Yes. He’s called Chris.’ She could feel her cheeks burning.

‘You need to end it now.’

‘Why?’ What chutzpa. What business was it of hers?

‘Marrying out doesn’t work. You need to find a Jewish boy. There are plenty out there who would suit you fine. I know a shidduch who could help you. You’re making a big mistake, Miriam.’

‘Am I?’ Miriam could feel her heart thumping, her skin prickle.

'This silly notion that there's one soulmate. It's nonsense. There are many men who could make you happy.'

'Really?' Miriam wondered why Ida had never married again after her husband died if there were so may suitable men out there. Her argument fell flat.

'Yes. You're breaking your parents' hearts. Listen to me. Do it now before it becomes too serious.'

Miriam saw before her an old woman whom nobody loved. Everyone felt duty to her, no affection. Her hair was short, her body plump, her clothes dowdy and beige.

'You can't tell me what to do, Ida.'

The old woman's face looked desolate. 'No, I can't. But I'm trying to stop you making a mistake for your own sake and for your parents. They are such good people. They don't deserve it.'

Miriam was livid: now Ida was using guilt and emotional blackmail. She burst into tears, dropped the laundry and left the room.

Miriam never told anyone about that conversation but the two women never spoke again. It was easy to bury their mutual loathing as Ida didn't talk much to anyone anyway and Miriam made sure that she never sat near her.

That night Miriam and Chris made love in the spare room with more passion than before: him fuelled by love and desire, her the same but also by defiance.

She'd made her decision and no-one - not even bitter, twisted Ida – could stop her.

17

Abby

I have so many bests.

My best friend is Devorah.

My best colour is purple.

My best song is 'Let it Go' from *Frozen.*

My best food is pizza.

My best weather is sunny.

My best place is with my family.

I love to dance and sing and it makes me happy when Mummy and Daddy, Leah and David clap and cheer for me. Then I feel like a shiny star.

One day I would like to be an actress and a singer but also a dancer.

Most the time I am happy: happy at my school, happy at my cheder, happy at home and happy with my zaider Harold (he is so funny) and my bubba Evelyn (she is a lovely granny but not a good cook). My other zaider and bubba live in Israel, a country far away, so I don't see them very often.

I like rainbows and glitter, sweets and stars.

The only things I don't like are snakes, lizards and Brussels sprouts. They are all green and slimy and I wish they weren't in the world.

I also don't like it when my brother and sister are moody but Mummy says that's what happens when you are a teenager and your body changes.

I'm not going to be a teenager and my body won't change. I like it just the way it is and I will stay the same for ever and ever. Shiny and sparkly like the stars.

Thank you for listening.

Amen.

Recipe: latkes or kugel (depending on how it goes)

Grate potatoes and onions.

Mix with matzah meal and egg.

Fry in little rounds in a pan.

If it all goes wrong, put it in a dish, roast until golden brown and call it kugel.

The party was drawing to a close, and the guests were getting ready to leave.

'Rebecca,' said her friend Esther. 'I just wanted to tell you that your latkes were so delicious I ate four of them.'

'You ate five,' responded Rebecca. 'But who's counting?'

18

Purim Fancy-Schmancy

Goldwell Hill's Shul took Purim seriously; or, rather, it was fun but you were expected to put a lot of effort into your costumes. It wasn't enough to don rabbit's ears and call yourself Bugs Bunny or carry a wand and declare yourself Tinkerbell. It required careful planning and there was another rule: each family or couple had to have a theme, although singletons could dress autonomously.

In the past, Miriam had felt that, due to their busy lives, their plans had been rather last minute but this year was different. Discussions started months before.

'What about Shakespearean characters? Antony and Cleopatra? Oberon and Titania?' she suggested as they finished another one of Chris' home-made curries one evening.

'I like that,' he said, ever loyal.

'So geeky,' said Hannah predictably, her mouth twisted in disdain. 'So academic.'

'Superheroes?' suggested Daniel. 'Star Wars characters? Star Trek?'

Hannah sighed and crossed her arms. 'Too weird.' What was wrong with her family? Why couldn't they be normal?

'Okay Hannah,' said Miriam. 'You make a suggestion then.'

The girl thought for a moment. Miriam looked at her seventeen-year-old. She was happy when she was with Taj but within the family home she could still be rather sulky, casting her shadow across any occasion. 'It has to be something which there are four of. The Beatles?'

'Brilliant,' said Miriam. 'There's that vintage shop in town that sells sixties clothes: we'll do that.'

The foyer of the shul was mayhem. The Steel family (John, Paul, Ringo and George) in their flares and sequinned waistcoats (Daniel a little self-conscious) met Harold and Evelyn (salt and pepper shakers), Morris - who always made his costumes food-related (this year, a pickled gherkin in green lederhosen and t-shirt with a sign: 'Mrs Ellswood: sweet and sour, but mainly sweet') - and Ida, whose only concession to the occasion was to wear a false moustache (although there was some slightly unkind debate among the youngsters as to whether it was fake or real). Ruth and family dressed as the characters from Little Red Riding Hood: Ruth (grandma), Simon (woodcutter), Leah (mother), Abby (Little Red Riding Hood) and David (the gentlest wolf ever to have prowled this earth).

There were families of crustaceans in pink plastic costumes (the rabbi had said it was alright to depict them, just not to eat them), several Elvis Presleys, and others from films: Dorothy from *The Wizard of Oz*, numerous Harry Potters and Hermione Grangers, and lots of generic Disney princesses.

The sight of film stars hugging crabs and wolves was bizarre but warming.

The seating in the shul had been rearranged so that, instead of the usual tiered rows, it was in the round with the bimah in the centre. Everyone took their seats although some (the giant lobster) found it harder than others to bend in the middle, and the story began.

Rabbi Woolf narrated the tale. He, his wife and three boys were dressed as Krispy Kremes, their rotund shapes perfectly suited to the foam circles that they had cut out and decorated with stick-on sprinkles.

'There was a king called Achashverosh,' he began in a deep tone,' (a boy duly appeared in a sheet tied with a cord and a cotton wool beard) 'and he commanded his wife Vashti' (out strutted a teenage girl, with a tendency to overact), 'to parade but she refused…' When it came to Esther, with Leah playing that role, Miriam felt a pang of jealousy that Hannah hadn't been asked to take the part; but of course they were infrequent attenders. She loved her niece but Leah, not Hannah, being chosen, reminded Miriam of how it felt as a child when Ruth was always selected, not her. History was stinging her again.

Every time the rabbi said 'Haman,' of course, everyone booed and shook their rattles and banged their tambourines and when he (unwittingly) chose his own manner of death, there were whoops and cheers.

Later there was a prize for the best costumes – the family of crustaceans won – and a lovely spread was laid out in the foyer with hamantaschen, latkes, doughnuts and sandwiches.

Afterwards, Rabbi Woolf had a meeting with Miriam and Ruth, Daniel and David (a Krispy Kreme, two Beatles, a grandmother and a wolf) about the forthcoming double-D barmitzvah, as it was now known. David was attending cheder and also had a private tutor to help him with the Hebrew but the rabbi wanted to check on Daniel.

'I'm teaching him the parashah,' said Miriam, sounding more confident about it than she felt.

The truth was that although she'd taught her children basic Hebrew, neither of them was that keen on it, deeming it too hard: the letters were strange and back to front. Every time she asked Daniel to work with her, he made excuses. He wanted to do the barmitzvah, he said, but he didn't want to put the effort in. He wanted to wake up on the morning and discover himself fluent. He had that slight leave-it-to-the-last-minute tendency of his father's - although when they wanted to do something and became absorbed, they did. Miriam didn't want any arguments with Daniel. This was just another stress to add to their already busy lives: Miriam and Chris' work, Chris' book (slow to evolve), Hannah and Taj, and life itself!

Their portion was Numbers 16, verses 1- 13 (Korach) about some of the rebels who rose up against Moses. The fact that these two gentlest of boys should have ended up with a passage about rebellion was ironic and rather amusing, but it was an interesting passage about power and greed. Miriam and Ruth had agreed that both their boys should learn the whole portion just in case one of them was ill or nervous and the other had to take over at the last minute. Of course, Miriam initially taught to it to Daniel with vowels, knowing that when they came to the actual reading from the scrolls, there wouldn't be any but hopefully he'd have learned it by then. The passage was especially hard at the start with names like Izhar and Korach, Dathan and Abiram.

Back at Harold and Evelyn's, the kids amused themselves while Miriam and Ruth discussed the forthcoming barmitzvah. It was clear that their styles (and budgets) were very different and that they'd both have to compromise.

'Of course, after the service there'll be kiddush. We'll just have the usual: dips, bagels with smoked salmon, challot, kiddush wine, grape juice and so on. Shall we just split the cost for that?'

'Of course.' Miriam could feel that Ruth was taking charge as if it were her domain and she was just subsidiary.

'Great. It's what to do for the party. Where to have it and so on.'

Miriam recalled Leah's batmitzvah in a lavish hotel with beautiful food, ice sculptures and strobe lighting, a live band and dancing. It was lovely but it must have cost a fortune and Chris, who was careful with money after a frugal childhood, wouldn't be happy with that expense: they couldn't afford it. Also, it wasn't their style.

'We could book the same hotel we had for Leah,' said Ruth as if tapping into Miriam's thoughts.

'Or maybe a barn that we could decorate ourselves?'

'The food there was really good.'

'Or we could do the catering ourselves with guests bringing salads and cakes.'

'The thing about a hotel,' persisted Ruth, 'is that they do the décor for you.'

'It would be lovely to do the decorating ourselves and put our own mark on it.'

Both women paused. There were clearly going to be tensions between them over taste, style and budget.

Evelyn called them in for dinner and the conversation was over, issues unresolved.

The atmosphere between the sisters remained frosty through dinner (a bit like Evelyn's undercooked chicken) but once the Steel family were back in their home, there was still the Friday night call:

'Shabbat shalom, Ruthie.

'Shabbat shalom, Mims.'

That was sacred; nothing altered it.

Being in London and seeing Rabbi Woolf again reminded Miriam that she and Daniel must work harder on his portion so it became a daily ritual, after dinner, to practise. Each evening, Hannah was either out with Taj or doing her homework, Chris would wash up and then work on his book, and Miriam and Daniel could settle to their task, at the now-cleared dining room table. The house took on a quiet stillness. Outside, daffodils trumpeted the golden spring and tiny pink blossoms sprigged the trees.

After a week, Miriam and Ruth decided to broach the issue of the reception again.

'Hi Mims.' Ruth spoke calmly on the phone, as if she were dealing with a slightly prickly customer at work. 'Rabbi Woolf has suggested that we use the shul hall for the reception. That will cut costs and we can decorate it how we like.'

'Or how the boys like,' said Miriam.

'Of course.'

And so that was sorted.

There were times in life when everything went wrong and others when everything was calm; this was the latter.

Of course, there was still the issue of confirming Hannah and Taj's relationship to the extended family. Was the barmitzvah really the right occasion?

Between Mehreen's home and Miriam's, about ten minutes apart, there was woodland. It was a great place for Hannah and Taj to meet. They loved its many bushes, large mature trees and you could be lost there, away from the world and its many issues. Religion and race were meaningless here. It was a land with no passport control, no prejudice, no borders.

They often met there in the early days of their relationship (long before it had been discovered) and liked to spend time in the den where Hannah and Daniel had played when they were young. They'd always called it The Laurel House: the way the bushes curved made it a sort of shelter or woody home. They'd never told their parents about it. It was their secret hideaway.

Now Hannah and Taj hid there and it was ideal. They could be a couple, taking food, drink and even books to read. It was a tree house on the ground, a refuge. It reminded Hannah of the succah they built each year as children, little foliage booths decorated with fruit where you could have your meals and even sleep, gazing up at the stars through the slatted branches. It was their own, leafy world. Hannah felt that she was a calmer, kinder person when she was with Taj, as if somehow he passed his serenity and wisdom onto her and that it was contained in this special place. With Daniel, it had been a play den. With Taj, it was a love nest. With Daniel, she was a girl. With Taj, she was a woman.

Daniel knew that he'd been usurped. He'd overheard Hannah several times on her phone whispering to Taj, 'Okay. I'll meet you in ten minutes at The Laurel House.'

Daniel had mixed feelings about Hannah using their secret retreat for meeting Taj. In a way it stung. He was left out. Being Hannah, she hadn't asked if he minded and he felt as if she'd evicted him from his home. On the other hand, it was more peaceful at home when Hannah wasn't there. There weren't so many screaming matches and tantrums when she was out. He had the house – and his parents - to himself, making him feel like an only child, not competing for attention.

Daniel told no-one about Hannah and Taj hiding out at The Laurel House. His sister would be livid if he did and there was no reason to disclose it – was there?

19

David

In a family like mine, you're expected to have special gifts, not special needs. That's the wrong kind of special. Of course, no-one ever says anything about it but I know what they must be feeling. They must be disappointed. The others in my family are clever and confident and they find life easy. I don't. They glide through life; I stumble through it.

Look at what they all do: my dad's got a really successful business. Mum's brilliant with numbers and works with Dad. Leah and Abby are so clever, they can do everything. My zaider Harold had a business. My bubba Evelyn is high up at her school. My uncle Chris is a lecturer. Aunty Miriam is a teacher. Great Uncle Morris is an accountant. My other Great Uncle Gerald is a scientist. Ida is an amazing sewer and so it goes on. Not only are they lovely people. They also know who they and what they want to be, whereas I don't really know what I am or who I want to be. My worst thing is when an old lady asks me, 'What would you like to do when you're older?' and I can't answer as I don't know. What I want to say is that I hope to be decent, honest and kind but that isn't what they are asking. They mean job, not character. They say everyone's got a talent but I don't seem to have one. I think God must have lost concentration when He was handing the gifts out and passed me by.

Ever since I can remember, I've found school work hard. The teachers at Hillel are great but when I'm taught new material it doesn't really sink in. I see the way that Leah and Abby work and it soaks into them, like a spillage on kitchen towel. They listen and absorb whereas I listen but it remains outside me.

It isn't just about school work. I go into a room full of people and I feel uncomfortable, embarrassed, guilty almost, as if I've done something wrong. I don't know why. I just haven't got that confidence gene. Leah and Abby can go on stage and sing and dance and talk to everyone but I can't. I feel self-conscious. I get tongue-tied. I don't know what to say.

Sometimes I worry about the future. I won't be able to be a doctor or lawyer or something brainy like that. I would like to take over my dad's business one day but I don't think I could. It's not just to do with being clever: it's about confidence and strength. My dad's quiet but he has this inner courage, like a mute lion.

I get on really well with my first cousin, Daniel. People call us Double-D as if we're twins. We're quite different, really: he's clever but shy. I'm also shy but not clever. We both have super-confident sisters who overshadow us. We both like sci-fi, dinosaurs, space, superheroes, making models, *Dungeons and Dragons*, *Star Trek*, wizards, magic: it's good to have someone who has the same interests as yourself.

When Mum told me her idea about having a joint barmitzvah, I wasn't sure as it made me look pathetic, like I couldn't manage it on my own. Everyone else does it alone but then, when I thought about it, it made sense. I was really anxious about it; so was Daniel. So I realised that we could help each other. It's like being in a choir. I don't mind singing in a group but I wouldn't want to sing a solo.

I hope the barmitzvah goes well. It is make or break. If we can manage it, everyone will be happy. If we don't – if I stumble – then I'll just feel like a failure again.

My family are everything to me. I do have some friends from Hillel, and the shul in Goldwell Hill but they are nothing compared to family. The way that my mum and dad support me. They never criticise; they only encourage. My sisters are annoying but I do love them. And my larger family too. My zaider and bubba are funny and sweet and Great Uncle Morris cracks me up with his jokes, even though some of them are a bit rude. He's more like a naughty schoolboy than a grown man.

At my – our – barmitzvah, we will have to say what being Jewish means to us and it's true. I'm proud to be Jewish. I like going to a Jewish school and living in a Jewish area as I don't have to explain who we are or what we do. People know why I can't play out at certain times or why we don't celebrate Christmas. On shabbat or at Chanukah, you can see the candles lit in the windows all down our street and it feels as if we are part of something big, something important and everyone understands it.

As if God is wrapping us in light and blessing us.

Daily.

Recipe: chremslach cremations

Put pieces of matzah in bowl.

Cover with hot water.

Add sugar, eggs, lemon juice, raisins.

Mix well.

Fry in oil.

Eat too many.

Book your cremation.

20

The big day approaches

The erratic summer weather seemed to mirror Miriam's moods: some days the sun was out, the sky was blue and unblemished and all seemed well. There were picnics and barbecues and Chris picked tomatoes and lettuces from the garden and prepared fresh salads. On other days, the grey clouds gathered and Miriam felt anxious and afraid. She still hadn't told her north London family about Hannah and Taj: if it fizzled out, what was the point in causing everyone upset and misery? Was that what she was secretly hoping for, she wondered?

Not that the relationship showed any sign of abating. Hannah and Taj seemed closer than ever and had even gone interrailing in Europe with a group of friends. Miriam had tried beforehand to broach the subject of contraception with Hannah but had been brushed off: 'I know all about that, Mum: we did it in PHSE.'

Many evenings after school and at weekends, Taj and Hannah sought refuge in The Laurel House. Their sanctuary meant so much to them, a place where they could kiss and be close, read and talk, opening their hearts to each other and confiding. Beneath the canopy of shiny leaves, they made their home from home. The more time went on, the more convinced they both were that this was love and that they were so lucky to have found each other.

Chris had almost finished his Shakespeare book and was getting ready to submit it to the publisher, then await a response. And Miriam's school year had come to a close. It had been a good one at Mounthill, the deputy Head Fletcher an ongoing irritant but otherwise fine. Even Lucas had made some progress and seemed happier.

Chris and Miriam went away for a few days on their own, to Suffolk. Hannah was on her Europe tour and Daniel had gone to stay with Ruth and family. It would be a good chance for the boys to prepare for the barmitzvah and help Daniel's confidence. He was always reluctant to go on school trips but was happy to go to family, especially with Harold and Evelyn, whom he adored, nearby.

'By the way,' said Miriam, as she dropped her son off at Ruth's house, 'I wouldn't say anything about Hannah and Taj just yet.'

'I won't,' said Daniel, rolling his eyes.

Suffolk was delightful: pink cottages with roses framing their doors; boats on the sea near Southwold; sweet-pea coloured houses framing the beach in Aldeburgh. Miriam and Chris walked, hand-in-hand, along the beach at Shinglestreet, marvelling at the sea-cabbages that grew randomly upon its stony surface and gazing out to a granite and flint sky.

In the evenings, they had fish and chips and sat on the low wall looking out to sea.

'Being here with you,' said Miriam, watching the gulls wheel noisily through the clouds, 'I feel that everything will be okay; but when we're back among all the issues we face, I'm not so sure.'

Chris smiled warmly at her. 'Everything's fine, Mimi. Life's up and down. It changes. It's never the same. We cope with it the best we can. Always together.'

Miriam wondered where his wisdom came from, his sanguine approach to life. She worried all the time, questioned, whereas Chris accepted, was calm.

'Poor Daniel,' she continued. 'With the big day coming up. Will it be too much for him? Am I putting him through it so that I can feel like a good Jewish mother?'

'Of course not. He wants to do it. He'll be fine.'

'And Hannah and Taj. Some days I feel ill thinking about the obstacles that they'll have to endure but then other days, I feel it's irrelevant what religion they are. All that matters is love.'

'I'd second that.' Chris reached out his hand and stroked his wife's.

'And Dad and his dodgy heart. Mum says that she's put him on this special diet but that he creeps down in the night and binges on pickles and chopped liver and empties the fridge.'

They both laughed.

'Your parents – they're great. So funny.'

That night, between soft white hotel sheets, they made love with more passion and feeling than for a long time before, as if declaring, once again, their undeniable commitment and love.

Returning home, they felt fresher and stronger than three days previously.

There was plenty to do. They all had haircuts; they picked up Daniel's suit (Ruth had bought the boys matching ties - not to Miriam's taste - but she decided not to argue about it), and Hannah and Miriam had a slight disagreement about what she should wear.

'I'm not an old granny with a skirt over my knees. I'm seventeen!'

'Yes, darling, I know but it's a synagogue service and so you have to look a bit demure.'

'Demure? I don't even know what that means. You're only worrying about what Bubbe and Ruth will say, let alone misery guts Ida.'

Later on, choosing her own outfit, Miriam remembered Hannah's words and realised that there was some truth to them. She was always torn between her desires and her obligations to others, who she wanted to be and who she felt she ought to be. She could wear one of her formal school suits (they all had to dress up for the annual Prize Day) or one of her artier dresses. She chose the latter (the blue would echo the theme well) but a longer one, below the knees: demure.

She and Daniel practised daily, sitting side by side at the kitchen table, her listening attentively to his gentle voice. He knew the portion well; also the brachot for the Torah, the Haftorah and the Ten Commandments in Hebrew. There was a lot to learn but he was doing brilliantly. She was proud of him, hoped he was doing it for himself, not just for her.

He was a lovely boy. Would life treat him well? Would he find love? Would he be fulfilled in his choices?

The day before the barmitzvah, they travelled down to London, the car full of clothes, books, papers; Miriam just hoped that they hadn't forgotten anything. Her palms were clammy, her heart racing.

That evening, Evelyn made one of her infamous shabbat meals (recipe 92: chicken with raisins, an uncomfortable combination) and they all sat together (Ruth and Simon were with his parents and Joel, just arrived from Israel.)

The atmosphere was excited, anticipatory with some anxiety on Daniel's part and also on Miriam's. Chris looked as calm as ever. Hannah was looking forward to seeing Taj the following day. Miriam thought it a shame that Morris and Ida always had to be there: appendages to any occasion. She didn't dislike them but they never seemed to change or develop. There was Morris telling another of his jokes:

'So...Esther and Ruth are in the car.

"Esther," says Ruth, "be careful: you've driven through two red lights and over a zebra crossing."

"Oh," says Esther. "Am I driving?" '

And when that failed to raise a laugh, he tried another:

'So…the police find Moishe drunk at three a m on the street.
"Where are you going?" they ask him.
"I'm attending a lecture on alcohol abuse and how it destroys marriages and families."
"At three a m? Who's giving the lecture?"
"My wife." '

And this time there were some giggles from the family while Ida looked sourly on.

Miriam put down her cutlery and thought for a moment: was *she* developing or changing? Not really. She was preoccupied with the same issues she'd always had. She really wanted to move forward.

Would the following day go well? Would the boys be confident enough?

And what about the revelation of Hannah and Taj? How on earth would that be received?

21

Chris

Growing up, I had this strange feeling that I'd been dropped from the sky into a random house. I'm so different from my parents that I was convinced that I'd been adopted. It was the *reverse* of the child who is given that news and is shocked. I was shocked *not* to be given that news.

We can't possibly be related. I'm tall and thin while my mum's petite and my dad's stocky. I know there are tall people in our extended family, though. I suppose I do have my mum's brown curly hair (although now it's grey) and maybe my dad's eyes but this is me searching hard for similarities rather than them being obvious.

If there are few physical similarities, there are even fewer interests in common. They are practical people: I'm not. They are get-on-with-it people; I dither. They are pragmatic; I'm a dreamer. We have different tastes in music, holidays, and food. I like reggae, France and curries. They like Val Doonican, Llandudno and roast beef. I've always loved books and reading but there are hardly any books in their home. My mum did always take me to the local library, as she felt she ought to, and maybe that's where my passion for reading started. I was allowed to take out as many books as I wanted (the librarian was so happy to encounter a kid in that area who actually wanted to read) staggering out with a huge pile which I devoured, swapping them a week later for more.

My mum and dad are modest and quiet, shy even. We never had people round for parties or meals. Maybe I'm also, at heart, slightly shy, but I enjoy lecturing and leading seminars. I suppose I'm confident in my subject. Also, my parents are Conservative with a small and big c. I am much more left wing and liberal about all issues: religion, sexuality, tolerance. The funny thing is that the three of us get on quite well, in a detached, civil kind of way, although we are worlds apart. I sometimes wonder if that's because we are essentially strangers and conflicts don't arise between loose acquaintances: they arise with people we care for, those we feel a deep connection with. 'Each man kills the thing he loves.'

I always found school work easy, especially the arts. It wasn't a very academic school but there was a group of us who liked the same activities - drama, music, literature - so we supported each other, sang in the choir, put on plays. University was even more liberating, being with like-minded people and feeling free to be myself was wonderful. A gift.

Meeting Mimi was the best thing that's ever happened to me. It was an instant attraction and we have so much in common. She's funny, beautiful, clever, impulsive, caring and loving. What more could anyone want? Once, I came back from a conference in the States and Mimi had lit candles along the drive leading to our door. Another time, she bought a dragon kite and we flew it on a beach in north Wales. She likes fireworks, sparklers, streamers and pinatas, which you fill with sweets, hang in the air, and hit with a stick until there's a candy shower. She loves to dance in her bare feet (even in the rain) and sing and be crazy. How I love her! How I value everything about her! Her thoughtfulness, her kindness, her spontaneity.

I wish she wouldn't beat herself up, though, and give herself such a hard time. Although she's such fun, she also suffers and struggles.

Much of her angst is about Judaism. It gives her great joy but also tremendous pain. She always wonders if she's being observant enough - or whether the children are - and what others will think. I feel sad about it because if she'd married a well-off, Jewish man as her sister did, then she could have lived in north London and have a community around her. She's quite unconventional so it would have had to be a Jewish writer or media type (Alan Yentob? Howard Jacobson? Amos Oz?) but then we wouldn't be together and we are soulmates and in love – still.

For me, Judaism is really positive. I don't carry the weight of its history on my shoulders as it is not my own religion although, of course, I'm interested in it. I like the family get-togethers, now that I'm used to several conversations going on at once, and I enjoy the warmth and conviviality. At first, I found it daunting, the noise, the mayhem, the expectation that you join in; but now I feel that I'm accepted for who I am and allowed to be myself. Harold and Evelyn have made me very welcome, even though in their hearts, I'm sure I wasn't their first choice as a son-in-law.

The only issue with which I struggled was Daniel's circumcision. Mimi and I spoke about it for ages and I know that she wasn't keen on it either but she did it for her parents' sake. Ruth, also, would have been horrified if she hadn't had it done. And if Daniel did want to live a Jewish life and marry in the faith, then it was deemed necessary. It just seems so strange to me. Why do you need to remove the foreskin of a child to make them Jewish? As far as I'm aware, it's a convention, a ritual, not a religious necessity. Also, you spend all your time as a parent protecting your child from harm and then you do that to them. It makes no sense. I found it very upsetting and Mimi and I both had tears in our eyes when it was carried out. Daniel cried and I'll never stop feeling guilty for the fact that I allowed him to be in pain. I should have been more defiant and refused to let it happen but I tend to quite passive. That's been a problem in my personal life and in work. I see other people get promoted but I don't.

Ruth! I didn't believe love-hate relationships existed until I met Mimi and Ruth. As an only child, I dreamed of having a sibling but when I see the two of them, I'm grateful for not having one. The fighting when they were young, Mimi tells me, was terrible: name-calling, hair-pulling, scratching and thumping. Thank goodness that's over. Now there's just a tension between them which feels palpable but that's all. They've grown up now and know, on the whole, how to behave. I really like Mimi's parents. Harold's fun and Evelyn's lovely although we always worry we've got food poisoning after her shabbat meals. For me, Judaism's very appealing: a warm light, surrounding and enveloping me.

I don't think it matters a jot who you marry, what colour or religion or gender they are. Who cares? Life's so short. All that counts is being happy and trying to lead a good life. I just want our kids to be fulfilled in their choices and lead worthwhile, positive lives.

My life seems to be a lucky one. I know that I do procrastinate with my work and I really struggled with that wretched Shakespeare book. The previous two, one on his sonnets, one on the histories, were well-received (and there have been some articles and papers at conferences) but this one was been slow going. To be honest, I'd rather be cooking a new curry for the family or digging up potatoes in the garden, but neither of those will get me a chair (Professor Korma? Professor Spud?) so I need to get on with my work. Maybe I'm a bit lazy.

Enough monologue.

Back to the book!

Recipe: Schnitzel, mitzel, as long as you've got your health

Take some chicken or veal.

Imagine your worst enemy.

Beat it with a rolling pin.

Dip it in breadcrumbs.

Fry till golden.

Eat and enjoy the taste of victory.

22

Barmitzvah Double D

The day before the big event, the two couples worked tirelessly to make the shul hall attractive. (The kids stayed with Harold and Evelyn.) Chris and Simon hung strings of bunting (white with blue Magen Davids) from one light fitting to another as well as clusters of white and blue balloons, like inflated bunches of grapes, from any hook they could find. Miriam and Ruth, meanwhile, put up the trestle tables and dressed them with stiff white cloths and napkins, and place settings, with flowers at the centre of each. The previously functional room looked joyful and bright.

Miriam was pleased with the venue: it was somewhere they all felt comfortable and it kept the cost down. In her heart, however, Ruth was disappointed. She felt bad that her son wasn't getting the lavish hotel function that Leah had had, but then she knew that it wasn't really David's style and it might overwhelm him so perhaps it was all for the best, after all.

Miriam could hear Chris and Simon making awkward small talk as they worked together. The men were so different and neither understood the world the other inhabited but they always tried hard, asking each other polite questions, as if their civility could help to smooth the sisters' prickly relationship.

'Business good?' asked Chris. (What on earth did Simon actually do? How was it so lucrative?)

'Your book progressing well?' asked Simon. (Did the world really need more books about Shakespeare? What new information could there possibly be?)

On this occasion, the sisters worked relatively harmoniously. There were, however, moments of tension: Ruth tending more towards formality and symmetry, Miriam to spontaneity, but they both trod carefully, compromising, conscious, all the time, that this day wasn't theirs but their sons', and therefore discussing each issue as it arose: should the cutlery be set in places or just put in the centre of each table? Should the name plates go on each plate or on the napkin? Should the cake be on display all the way through the reception or just brought in at the end?

As they worked together it occurred to Miriam how close the sisters were and yet how far apart. In some ways they felt so connected; in others they were strangers. Their contrasting appearances not only confirmed this strange duality but also symbolised how different their homes and lifestyles were. Ruth's smart, tidy hair and dress sense revealed her organised home (not even a teaspoon out of place in her clinical kitchen) and her clearcut, decisive attitude to life. Miriam's shaggy hair, many bangles and rings, and love of flowing patterned clothing were outward demonstrations of what her home was like – chaotic, homely but messy – and her lifestyle: random, disorganised.

By ten o'clock that night, the room was set out perfectly (a bit stiff and formal for Miriam's taste but she didn't comment) and they all left, Simon and Ruth to their house and Chris and Miriam to her parents'. The sisters had managed the day without argument: it felt like a miracle. Both felt tired, relieved and secretly gave themselves credit for avoiding conflict.

The next morning, there was a tingling anticipation in the air as before a wedding: everyone showered; clothes stiff with newness; shoes polished; flowers delivered in a large box and a sense of excitement.

Driving to the shul, Miriam prepped her parents:

'I told you that Hannah's bringing her boyfriend today, so you'll meet him.'

'Who?' said Harold.

'Shush, Harry,' said Evelyn, straightening his tie. 'Your granddaughter.'

Miriam caught Hannah's eyes in the rear view mirror and winked at her.

She and Chris had talked endlessly about how, where, and when and had decided that this would be a good opportunity. Mehreen and her family would attend the barmitzvah, as old friends of theirs, and among the joy and fun, it would all be accepted as part of the happy day. Hopefully.

Now Miriam wasn't so sure.

The two families arrived early at the shul, as planned, to meet Rabbi Woolf who was standing in the foyer, amiable as ever, to greet them.

'Good morning,' he said, 'gut shabbos. Big day today, boys,' and he patted them each kindly.

Daniel and David stood shoulder to shoulder and smiled nervously. They both wore suits (chosen by their mums), their ties more jolly than they were, striped blue and white. (Miriam still didn't like the ties that Ruth had chosen for them – they looked like trainee accountants – but she kept schtum.)

And then the guests started arriving: Israel and Gretel looking increasingly frail; Morris; Ida; the Wood family with their twins, Jacob and Saul; Mehreen and her family (they'd stayed overnight in London with her sister); Harold and Evelyn already there; Simon's parents from Israel and their son Joel, who was in a wheelchair and seemed dazed. Evelyn still wished that Gerald and his family would attend but she knew that they wouldn't.

Maureen and Ian looked out of place, her in a hat, skirt and jacket, dressed more for communion than kiddush. They'd never been to a synagogue before and felt some trepidation about it, even though Chris had explained: the prayer books open back to front; they are written in Hebrew and English; Daniel and his cousin David would be reading from a huge scroll. As he spoke, they looked bewildered as if he were saying, 'We are entering a world of unicorns, horsemen and bare-breasted mermaids. Join in!' He kept the description of Judaism limited, not mentioning circumcision, the blowing of rams' horns and eating an apple and nut paste to symbolise mortar. That would have made them even more uncomfortable. They looked nervously around them as if they'd landed in a brothel or an acid house and wished they could leave.

There were the regular congregants and colleagues, family friends and the boys' mates too. Miriam knew that there would be more people there for her sister than her: that was inevitable as Ruth was so involved with the shul and Miriam had moved away over twenty years before. She was starting to realise that wherever she was, she was always on the margins, a maverick: at school, at shul, in the family even. It seemed to be her destiny to be peering through the window from outside, her nose pressed against the glass, whereas Ruth was always inside, belonging.

Everyone took their seats, the families near the front. Chris placed his parents behind him, as if he were their shield. Miriam turned around, receiving a warm smile from Mehreen. One of the many qualities that she loved about Goldwell Hill Synagogue was that everyone was welcome: she could see families, single people, a gay couple, black Jews, Golda in a wheelchair, Barry with his guide dog. They were all genuinely included. It didn't matter that Chris was one of the few men wearing only a kippa and no talit: no comment would be made. He'd been to shul a few times now and was quite used to its conventions: the standing up and sitting down; turning to face the Torah scroll when it was processed; not eating or drinking anything at the kiddush until the brachot were made.

Miriam also liked the way that everyone had made an effort to look smart and colourful but it wasn't a fashion show and there was no competition. Few women wore hats. A couple of them wore a talit and kippah but most didn't. Miriam and Ruth had agreed to wear blue but they looked very different: Ruth in a smart turquoise skirt and jacket, Miriam in a flowing Indian style dress with blues and whites in swirly patterns. Simon wore a suit that he often wore to work; Chris was in a grandfather shirt, chinos and a jacket. He hated ties.

Rabbi Woolf stood on the bimah and welcomed them all.

'Family and friends. We are here today to witness a very special celebration for two fine young men, Daniel and David, an event we in the know have coded Barmitzvah Double D - but I can assure you no lingerie is involved.' Everyone laughed and the rabbi winked at David and Daniel, both of whom looked apprehensive. David's face was flushed; Daniel had curled his notes into a cylinder. 'Our service today starts with 'Mah Tovu'. Please stand.'

The singing was fulsome and whole-hearted. Miriam had always loved the music at services, especially when she could feel the camaraderie and good intentions swelling within the notes. She felt that the congregation was willing the boys on. Daniel stood between her and Chris, and Hannah was beside her. The row Miriam had had with her over her dress being rather short had abated: in the end, Miriam relented. The irony was that Hannah was now trying to tug the skirt down as if she felt exposed by it, perhaps regretting her choice, although she'd never admit it. She hadn't thought about the fact that when she sat down, the skirt rode up. Behind Miriam were Harold and Evelyn, feeling proud. Evelyn was looking round, curiously, for signs of Hannah's boyfriend but couldn't see him anywhere. Maybe he'd been unable to come, after all.

On the other side of the bimah were Ruth and family with Simon's parents and Joel in his wheelchair behind. He looked a bit restless and was muttering to himself, shaking his head from time to time. Masha and Adam looked strained: the flight from Israel had been delayed and Joel had been agitated. They each tried continuously to soothe him, placing their hands on his shoulders.

The service rolled along as it always did with Rabbi Woolf, smoothly. You were in safe and loving hands.

When the boys were called up, Daniel could see that David was shaking and was even more nervous than him and so he whispered, 'Let's smash it.' It made David smile.

They sang the blessing on the Torah together, standing shoulder to shoulder, and then Daniel, as previously agreed, read the first half with the difficult names and then David took over. Daniel's reading was more legato, David's more staccato (he stumbled twice) but they moved through slowly and steadily, egged on by the other. Then the blessing after reading from the Torah and everyone shouted 'Mazal tov' and 'Shecoyah!'

The Haftorah went well as did the reading of the Ten Commandments which, again, they shared. Both boys relaxed as time went on. The relief was evident on their faces.

But it was their d'var Torah which most members found moving and which they would remember for years to come. It was typed up and prepared but they read it with panache. There was humour: 'Well, we haven't rebelled yet but a warning to our parents, we may start soon,' and deeper reflections: 'This passage teaches us that being power hungry just for the sake of it is not advisable. Look at Korach and the other rebels: the earth swallowed them up as their punishment.'

They stood by the Ark and read the Prayer for a Barmitzvah, their parents by their side: 'May we be true Bnei Mitzvah, sons of the commandment…'

After the service, the boys led kiddush and then the meal began. That was when the relief and fun came. The boys were on a youngsters' table with their siblings and friends: Jacob and Saul, Hannah, Leah and Abby, Taj and Jamil and other barmitzvah boys in David's cheder class.

The boys' parents and grandparents were on another table and Morris was, once again, on the miscellaneous pick-and-mix with Ida, a widow, a widower, two divorcees, Golda in her wheelchair and Barry with his dog. The meal was a buffet. (Ruth had recommended the caterers.) Everyone went up, table by table, to help themselves to the wonderful array of food: salmon, fish balls, many different salads, bowls of new potatoes shiny with butter, and then a delicious array of desserts and coffee.

It was when everyone had their plates full that Morris chose his moment: 'So…' he began, 'Moishe opens the bedroom drawer and sees five nuggets and two gold eggs. "What's this?" he asks Rebecca. She sighs. "Well, over the years I've had a few flings (who hasn't?) and each time I had an affair, I bought a gold egg." Well, thinks Moishe: two eggs in forty years. "Fair enough," he says. "What about the nuggets?" "Each time I had five eggs I swapped them for a nugget." '

Barry laughed, the dog barked and Golda chuckled but Ida remained stony-faced. Morris and his perennial jokes. He thought life was one big laugh. Wasn't it time that he realised it wasn't?

Simon stood up and gave a speech thanking everyone who'd helped prepare the boys (Chris had been invited to say a few words but declined: he was used to public speaking but felt that this wasn't somehow his domain) and then the klezmer band, Mazal Tov, arrived and the dancing began.

It was mainly the younger guests who danced, in a circle, in concentric circles and alone or in pairs, doing the chora. Mostly the older guests sat at the side tables, drinking wine, clapping and cheering, although Morris did have a couple of dances until he was out of breath and had to back out. Maureen and Ian stood up to dance but their waltz was out of pace with the fast rhythm and so they sat down again, breathless.

Harold was worn out: since the heart attack, he'd noticed that he had much less energy than before. The cardiologist kept saying that he was 'in fine nick' but he didn't feel the way he used to. Evelyn, beside him, was bemused: where was Hannah's boyfriend? And then, gradually, she worked it out. It was Taj, their Muslim friend. She noticed the couple touching hands under the tablecloth, the close dancing and the embrace later on when they didn't know they were being watched. It came as a shock. Could Miriam not have prepared her? Wouldn't that have been better?

It made Evelyn feel confused: her religion sometimes did that to her. She was always analysing, thinking, trying to work out answers where none was provided. She'd nothing against Taj (she knew that Miriam and Mehreen were great friends) but it was yet another tricky issue. Miriam always seemed to make life difficult. Ruth had made easier, more consistent decisions. It didn't free her from all problems but the foundation of her life was more solid. With Miriam, there were always quandaries, and here was another one. Evelyn could foresee only difficulties ahead. Her heart sank.

The perfect day had come to a bewildering end for her. She worried about Miriam, and about Hannah and about Taj. How would his extended family feel? Theirs?

Evelyn knew that Miriam agonised about her Judaism, how to retain it whilst living with others. Now there was another dimension to it and the agonising would continue. It never ended.

Miriam saw Ruth watching Hannah and Taj dancing together and she knew that she knew. Ruth's face was ashen. The shock hit her like cold water. Whey had Miriam allowed this to happen?

At about one a.m. the band stopped. The napkins and tablecloths were crumpled and stained with grape juice and wine; the food was eaten; the guests had gone and Harold looked grey with tiredness.

'I'm taking your father home,' Evelyn said to her daughters, her arms around them both. 'Thank you for a wonderful day.'

'It was great, wasn't it?' said Miriam.

'Perfect,' said Ruth.

'Yes,' said Evelyn. 'Perfect.'

23

Hannah

Being Jewish in a non-Jewish area isn't easy. It was simpler for Mum growing up in north London. I've had some name-calling at school: 'big nose,' 'stingy', 'has your brother had his willy sliced?': the same stereotypes which are just silly. It's ignorance. I know that but it's still not very pleasant and it pisses me off. Seriously.

I think that's one of the things that Taj and I have in common: we know what it's like to be a member of a minority. But that's not all that binds us. We both love studying and music and the environment and our families are great friends. Our values are the same. We both feel passionately about things – and each other. He makes me a better person.

I know that Mum worries about me being with a Muslim, but that's just her generation which is hung up on difference. We don't see it that way. We know that love conquers all and, anyway, she didn't marry someone Jewish so it's a bit of a cheek to expect me to. Honestly! You can't want your children to make up for your mistakes. It's not fair.

Taj and me: it just happened naturally. We didn't plan it.

Mum knows who she is on many levels: a loving wife, good mum, great daughter and sister, teacher, book-lover, but she's so confused about religion and she's passed that angst onto us. It's not fair. Part of her wants to be Jewish, married to a Jew, living in north London (like Ruth); and then another part of her wants all religion to go away and let us all mix and mingle. Honestly, she's so confused. She wants Jewish people to stay apart; then she wants them to integrate. That's her dilemma. It's not right to pass that issue down. It pisses me off. Seriously.

I haven't got that hang-up. I'm me. I have a Jewish heritage and a Christian heritage and I'm in love with a Muslim. It doesn't matter. Get over it! I've got my own unique identity and, if others don't like it, they can sod off, as far as I'm concerned. I'm not being funny but there's no way that I am going to let this hang over me all my life. If I have kids (and I'm not sure I want them anyway) they won't carry my problems on their backs. They'll make their own lives and their own decisions and I'll support them. End of.

My generation believes in the right to be yourself, unchained. Lead your own life, not someone else's. Daniel wanted a barmitzvah. I didn't want a batmitzvah. That's my choice and nobody else's. What does it matter?

We know that it's wrong to discriminate because of gender, race, colour of your skin, belief, sexuality. None of these should count against you. They are private issues. No-one else has the right to judge you on them. It really hacks me off.

In the past, there was terrible racism, antisemitism, homophobia. We're better than that now. Kids know that those prejudices are wrong. What makes me laugh is they always say that the young need educating in these areas but we know it already. It's the old who need educating. Older people are much more narrow-minded than we are. Take my great-granny Gretel. She seems like a nice old lady and she always sends Daniel and me money at Chanukah but she's racist. She also makes comments about gay people even though her son, my uncle Morris, is gay. Outrageous! How must that make him feel? I think it's out of order. Seriously.

My Aunt Ida's no better. She frowns at people who aren't Jewish enough. It's none of her business, moody old cow. It's only 'cos she's lonely and sour. She should make her own life and stop judging others.

I have great hope for the world because the young are the future and their values about the environment, sexuality and race are spot on.

We've got it sorted.

The world will be a better place when this generation's in charge.

Seriously.

Recipe: Teiglach

In one bowl, mix eggs, oil and water.

In another bowl, mix flour, salt and baking powder.

Combine the two.

Make the dough into balls and bake.

In a third bowl (keep up) mix honey, sugar and orange juice.

Pour the syrup over the balls.

Lose a filling or a crown.

Book an emergency appointment with the dentist.

24

The Aftermath

'It was such a great day,' said Evelyn. She and Miriam were on the phone, the morning after the barmitzvah.

'I thought so too, Mum.' She could hear Chris and the kids laughing in the garden. He had the hose out and was spraying them; they were shrieking, pretending to care when they got wet.

'The boys were amazing, the food delicious. Everyone enjoyed it. It was all lovely.'

'I agree.' Miriam waited. She knew that her mother would want to make positive comments before the criticism: build the house of cards, then knock it down. After all, she was a teacher with years of report writing experience: begin with praise, then suggest areas for improvement.

'Why didn't you warn me, Miriam? Us?'

Miriam sat down on the stairs by the phone and sighed. 'Oh Mum. I didn't know whether it was going to last or not and so there seemed no point in telling you before. You've had so much to worry about with Dad's health and work and I knew that you wouldn't approve anyway.'

'It's not a matter of approval, Miriam. Hannah has to make her own decisions. It's her life and Taj is, I'm sure, a lovely young man but they're setting themselves up for so many difficulties with family and society. They're choosing a very hard path and you, more than anyone, should know that.'

'I know.' Miriam could feel tears prick her eyes, felt stung by her mother's rebuke. 'But they're in love and what can I do? If I tell her not to see him again she might really rebel so I can't.'

'No, of course not. She's very headstrong.'

'Like me?'

Evelyn laughed. 'Yes, just like her mum.'

There was a pause in which mother and daughter thought carefully, deeply, not wanting to blame or hurt or say things that they'd later regret.

'Part of me feels that she's got the right to make her own decisions and we've raised our kids not to have prejudice towards others' race or religion but part of me also agrees with you.'

There was a pause. Miriam knew that her mother would think carefully about what she said.

'It's very hard, sweetheart.'

'I've let you down.' The tears were slipping down Miriam's cheeks now. She could feel herself descending into bleakness.

'No. You haven't, but one thing leads to another. Where you live, who you marry, determines everything. It all follows on.'

Miriam felt chastised by her mother's words.

'I understand that but I still want my children to be citizens of the world. I do really believe in that. I can just imagine what Ruth will say.'

Evelyn didn't answer. There was nothing she could add.

The following week, Miriam, Ruth and Evelyn met for lunch. Hannah was with Taj; Chris and Daniel were spending the day together at home. It was Ruth's suggestion that the three women convened and Miriam felt as if she'd been summoned, having no choice but to accept. There was that slight feeling of being called by the headmaster to his office.

They met at an Italian restaurant in Covent Garden which they all liked, a vine draped over a trellis above their heads like a scarf on a giant mannequin. The walls had frescoes of Florence, Rome and Pisa with cracks painted on to make them look old. The napery was stiff and white, the glasses catching the light in their polished curves.

They ordered vegetarian options, to avoid any kosher issues.

The waiter placed a large wooden platter upon their table: antipasti varnished by oil: artichoke hearts; panini and bruschetta; olives and capers dotted around; cherry tomatoes stuffed with soft cheese. The women drank sparkly mineral water in tall glasses, the ice and lemon colliding with each other in their confined space.

'The double barmitzvah was such a success,' said Ruth and Miriam thought how like Evelyn she'd become, prefacing bad news with good. 'Everyone has said so.'

'Oh absolutely,' agreed Miriam and Evelyn nodded.

'How are the family?' asked Ruth. Miriam noticed that the longer her own hair grew, the shorter Ruth's became, as if she was differentiating herself from her sister – or was she imagining that?

'All well, thank you.' Miriam knew that Ruth was really asking about Hannah and Taj so she stubbornly delayed giving that information till last. 'Chris' book is with the publishers now, Daniel's enjoying the summer, as am I, before school starts again and Hannah's still going strong with Taj.' There: they had it. That's what they wanted. That's why they were there.

As they all transferred the food from the board to their plates and then their mouths, making sure that they took only their fair share, the honesty began. Miriam was expecting it but was still shocked by the sharpness of the delivery.

'You need it put a stop to it,' said Ruth bluntly.

Evelyn tried to soften the atmosphere and Ruth's words. 'What Ruth means, darling, is that maybe you should talk calmly to Hannah about the situation.'

'I have.' Miriam could feel herself being defensive, as she always was under attack. She put her cutlery down. She'd suddenly lost her appetite. 'Do you really think that I haven't?'

'And what does she say?'

'That she loves him and that race and religion don't matter and in a way I agree with her.'

'The problem is,' said Ruth, removing an olive stone from her mouth and placing it carefully at the side of her plate, 'that you've given her mixed messages, Miriam.' Ruth's tone was sharp. 'You say that it's fine and then not fine. If one of my kids, God forbid, did what she's done, I would stop it straightaway. It wouldn't be acceptable. Finished.'

'She's seventeen, Ruth.'

'I don't care. She doesn't know what's good for her. You do. You're the adult. The problem is that you're confused about what you think and therefore, so is she.'

Miriam could feel tears in her eyes. She had the stem of a caper stuck in her throat and was coughing.

Evelyn poured her daughter some sparkling water and passed the glass to her. 'Girls. Let's keep this pleasant. We're trying to help you, Miriam.'

’Are you?’ Miriam cleared her throat, tried to make her voice strong. ‘Or are you just pointing out, once again, that I’ve fucked up?’

Evelyn bristled at the profanity. Two women at the neighbouring table raised their eyebrows before returning their attention to their tortellini.

‘Why don’t you just say it? I married out and moved to the Midlands and therefore my kids don’t feel very Jewish and my grandchildren won’t either. I did the wrong thing. You, of course, Ruth, did the right thing, as always. Mazal tov, Ruth. You win again.’ Miriam lifted her glass in a mock toast.

‘Girls,’ said Evelyn, her cheeks reddening. ‘This isn’t the pleasant conversation we wanted. We’re all adults now.’

‘It’s always been the same,’ said Miriam, standing up now, her crumpled napkin falling to the floor. ‘Ruth’s the success story. I’m the disappointment. We all know that.’

‘Miriam - ’

‘How dare you both make me feel so utterly miserable?’

‘Darling -’ started Evelyn, trying to placate.

With fumbling hands, Miriam found twenty pounds in her purse and threw it on the table to cover her share and then ran out of the taverna.

All the way back - on the tube, the train and her car, which she’d parked at the station - tears streamed down her cheeks.

As soon as she arrived home, Chris could see that she was very upset. Hannah was in the garden with her dad and Daniel. She'd been out with Taj but was now back and Chris had made them home-made milkshakes in tapered, frosted glasses.

'What happened?' he asked, coming into the house, concerned. His wife's cheeks were smeared with tears.

'It's Ruth and Mum. They criticised me. They think that we should forbid Hannah from seeing Taj.'

'That's crazy.' Chris wanted to say: what a cheek! It's none of their business! But he'd learned that criticising Mimi's family - even though she did so - could repeat on him, like bile.

'They say that Hannah's Jewish and that she doesn't know that she's making a mistake and that we're being weak to allow it.'

'That's nonsense.'

'I need to talk to Hannah.'

'Ok but calmly, please. Daniel and I will go and get us fish and chips. Have a quiet discussion with her, please Mimi. She's in such a good place at the moment.'

Miriam thought: no wonder Chris' personal tutees always say how great he is: patient, measured, a conflict-avoider.

Miriam found Hannah in the garden, painting her fingernails. She was in a deck chair, knee bent up, head bowed to the task, her face obscured by her dark curls. She dipped the tiny brush into the bottle and dabbed the crimson colour carefully on.

'Hi Mum. How was London?'

'Okay. Hannah, I want to talk to you, sweetheart.'

Hannah's dark eyes narrowed defensively, but she didn't look up. 'Oh yes? What about?'

'You and Taj.' Hannah's shoulders dropped. She put the brush back in its bottle and stared at her mum.

'I see. Bubbe and Aunty Ruth have had a go, have they?'

'No. Not a go, exactly. They just feel - and so do I - that although Taj is a delightful boy, mixing Judaism and Islam doesn't work.'

'Well, it does for us.' Her tone of voice escalated from warm to defensive to angry.

'You think it does now -'

'That's total hypocrisy. What about you and Dad?'

'That's different. He doesn't have his own religion. Taj does. It's not going to work out, Hannah. It needs to stop before -'

'Before what?' Hannah was standing up now, her face red. 'You're being racist. You always told us not to be.'

'That's not racist, darling.'

'Then what else is it? If he was white and Jewish you'd like him. You're judging him simply on his race and religion.'

'I forbid it,' said Miriam, hearing her mother and sister's language in her mouth, as if she were a ventriloquist's dummy, and feeling that the words were alien to her.

'Oh do you? Right,' said Hannah and she stormed off, out of the garden, up to her room where she packed a holdall and left the house, slamming the front door behind her.

Miriam sat on the garden chair, stunned, unable to move. Time lost its meaning. The large yellow courgette flowers and the blushing tomatoes stared at her, accusingly. The garden spun.

She heard the car drive up; then Chris and Daniel came into the garden, carrying wrapped paper bundles, like swaddled babies. She could see grease spotting the paper.

'Where's Hannah?' asked Chris, the colour draining from his previously tanned face.

They searched her room and could see that some of her clothes were missing. Her charger and phone weren't on the desk, where she usually kept them.

Miriam rang her phone. It went to voicemail.

'Hannah, darling. It's Mum. I'm sorry I upset you. Please ring me back and we can talk. I'm worried about you.'

The boys ate their fish and chips in the garden, Miriam unable to eat, Hannah's portion still unwrapped.

Later, Daniel buried himself in a computer game. Chris stood by Miriam, looking concerned. 'Ring Mehreen,' he said.

'Mehreen? It's Miriam here. Sorry to bother you -'

'Miriam. Taj has gone. He's packed a bag, taken his pocket money and left. We're beside ourselves.'

'Hannah too. Where are they, do you think?'

'I don't know. He isn't answering his phone. Shall we ring the police?' Miriam could hear the quiver in her friend's voice. How would she feel when she discovered that it was Miriam who'd driven her away?

'No. Leave it. I'm sure they'll come back soon.'

The sunny day turned to an overcast evening: then came the darkness of night. Miriam didn't sleep. Nor did Chris. They waited for the phone to ring.

It didn't.

25

Daniel

The way I see it, we're all boats sailing on a vast sea. Some have an easy journey, floating along without a care. Others have a more difficult time, on choppy waters, struggling.

Hannah's in the first group; I'm in the second. We can wave to each other and are connected to some extent but we're very different. She'll glide through life, doing what she wants to do. You could call it selfish or you could just say that she has a strong sense of who she is.

In a way, I envy her. For me, each day's a challenge. It's hard to explain, as others would probably say that I'm clever, but nothing comes easily to me. What I do achieve is through hard slog and graft. I am not just talking about work. Everything.

We go to lots of family dos, which are pleasant in a way but they're also stressful 'cos you're meant to join in and be part of it, express an opinion, but I don't find it easy. Then there's sport where you have to be in a team; friendship's the same. You're meant to fit in, find a place to slot into like a coin in a parking machine.

In that way, I find it easier with my nana and grandad Steel. Their house is quiet and peaceful and you aren't expected to say anything clever. You can sit and eat your meal but it's not an awkward silence. It's a comfortable one and I feel at peace there. They accept me. With bubbe and zaider Green, you're meant to say your piece, tell what you've been up to, share your news, give an opinion. It's warm and loving but it's not easy. Great Uncle Morris manages it by telling jokes, some of them quite rude and Great Aunty Ida sits and frowns. It's crazy, really, the way we deal with life. In a way, I can see why Gerald just opts out.

Poor David. It's even worse for him because he struggles at school and has trouble forming his ideas. I don't have the same issues in that way. We're lucky that we're first cousins as we get on really well. I'm not saying we're exactly the same but we understand each other. People tend to pair us together in that Double D joke as if we're twins but we're not. In some ways, he has it easier than me as he's closer to the family, but I have it easier in that I do well at school so at least there's one area I succeed in. But we sense when the other is struggling and give each other time. We can play computer games together or watch a film and there's no need to talk. We're happy like that, side by side.

We smashed the barmitzvah. Everyone was proud. It felt good that the family was pleased. Maybe this Jewish thing is more interesting than I'd realised. I might like to get more involved in the future but I'm not sure. I'll see how it goes.

Hannah's with Taj now. I don't know if they'll stay together but they seem strong. Mum would probably like me to marry someone Jewish but there aren't any Jewish girls around here so it's a bit hard to find them. It's not really fair that the pressure's on me because Hannah's done the so-called wrong thing. It's like, if she's rude to Mum and Dad and they're upset, I have to be extra-well-behaved to compensate and that's not on.

Hannah and I used to be really close but we've grown apart. She can be a moody cow sometimes. You can tell she's in a bad way when her skin gets spotty and she crosses her arms and scowls like a dragon. When we were younger, we had a special den, The Laurel House, in the local park. It was an area where no-one else seemed to go. The trees happened to be arched to make a space where we sat and read, played, took snacks and made a second home. We even hung our clothes on protruding branches and we really liked escaping there.

We never told Mum and Dad about The Laurel House. It was our secret, our private space, and we felt comfortable there. So I felt pretty annoyed when she told me that she and Taj were using it to meet. I was also really angry when I realised that she'd stolen my money. Mum and Dad give us some each week and I was saving up for some Star Wars Lego that David and I were going to build. Hannah's always going on about the environment and equality like she's a saint but she's selfish, only thinking about herself.

There's a girl, Lisa, who I like but I haven't told anyone. She's pretty and clever but everyone likes her so I wouldn't stand a chance anyway. Sometimes, when I want to speak, the words don't come easily to me. In that way, I'm more a Steel than a Green.

The Greens have language pouring from their mouths like fountains. The Greens can express themselves, remember jokes, tell stories, comment, commiserate, congratulate. They always have their words ready, as if they'd swallowed a dictionary. The Steels stumble and stutter. Language makes them uncomfortable. They prefer silence, without pressure to perform.

I'm good at English on the page, like Mum and Dad. I get good marks for my essays and creative writing but when it comes to speaking, it doesn't flow easily from me. It's like there are two English languages, the written and the spoken. I'm good at one and rubbish at the other. I'll try and get a job which involves writing, not speaking.

Maybe I'll be a speechwriter. Then I can write down my ideas but not have to stand and deliver them. Someone else can do that. That would be ideal.

The women in our family are chatterers. The men are quieter, apart from Morris but then he's not really revealing himself. He's just reciting jokes, like a script, which he's heard before, as if he's wearing a mask: getting laughs without anyone knowing who he really is.

I think a lot about life. I don't say as much as Hannah but that doesn't mean that I'm not thinking. In fact, my brain's working most of the time. I wake often at night, my head buzzing: ideas, questions, topics.

So much to think about.

So much to decode.

Recipe: Bagels

Mix flour, yeast, egg and water in a bowl.

Wait till it rises.

Shape the dough into rounds.

Stick your finger in each one to make a hole.

Boil the bagel, not your finger.

Serve.

The optimist sees the circle; the pessimist, the hole.

It's the Jewish version of the glass half empty or full.

What do you call Jewish seabirds?

Baygulls.

26

The Wandering Jew and Muslim

Miriam stayed awake all night, pulling back the bedroom curtains and staring hopelessly into the hollow darkness, finding no comfort there. She checked her phone, warm from being held in her hand, a hundred times but nothing from Hannah. She left several voice messages for her daughter but received no reply. Chris tried to stay awake to keep his wife company, but he kept slipping helplessly into sleep, escaping the situation.

Next door, Daniel slept soundly. He knew that his sister was with Taj and that she was safe. He saw her dramatic absconding as her jealousy that the attention had been on him for once, at his barmitzvah. It annoyed him: she always had to be in the spotlight and now it was on her again. Silly cow.

Miriam felt a mixture of nausea and emptiness. Bile rose through her mouth and made her tongue taste acidic. Her heart was pounding, her mind racing. Where was Hannah? Was she in danger? Was she being kept against her will? Was she even alive?

She sent her a string of loving messages: *Hannah, darling, please let me know that you are okay…Hannah sweetie. I love you. Please contact me…Hannah, my love. You are not in any trouble. Please come home.*

No reply.

Then suddenly at seven the next morning, the phone beeped. It was from Hannah: *We are safe. We just need some space.*

‘Chris, Chris,’ Hannah rocked the duveted lump that was her husband. ‘I’ve had a text. They’re okay.’

‘I said they were,’ opening one sticky, sleepy eye, which he then closed and slept again.

Miriam rang Mehreen.

‘Mehreen, sorry to wake you.’

‘You haven’t. I’ve been awake all night, worrying and crying.’

‘Me too. Have you had the message?’

She had. They read the same words to each other as if they were a sacred text that they could share: ‘If you prick us, do we not bleed?’ Miriam thought: here we are, a Jewish mother and a Muslim mother and we both feel exactly the same, as if we are of one mind, one heart.

‘We can’t call the police now. They’ll say that they’re not missing or being held against their will. We know that they’re not in danger.’

‘That’s true.’

Both women sobbed, staying on the phone to listen to and support each other. Miriam recalled an inset day at school when a counsellor had talked to the staff about supporting teenagers in crisis. She’d said that we, in our society, are uncomfortable with people crying so we try to stop it: have a tissue, wipe your eyes, don’t cry, it will be alright. But actually the best thing you can do is to let someone cry and stay with them, not be embarrassed.

Maybe Mehreen remembered that inset day too as the two women let each other cry, the sobbing the only sound, connected by a phone line and a very deep friendship.

The next few days were seamless. Night and day indivisible. Time had no meaning. August was usually a lovely time for the family: no school or work, (although Chris always had some article or paper that he was working on and trying to avoid writing). The days were long and sunny, time spent with family and friends, light salad meals and barbecues.

But this year was different. Miriam waited all day for another message from Hannah but there was nothing. She was very relieved that Ruth and her family were in Israel visiting Simon's folks (they'd now built a large annex onto their house in Tel-Aviv where the five of them could stay more often) and Miriam hadn't told her parents. The last thing she wanted was to cause her dad more strain.

Her mum had rung one evening and she'd had to put on an artificially happy voice.

'Is everything alright, darling? Enjoying the summer holidays?' Evelyn asked, suspiciously. Something didn't feel right.

'Yes fine,' said Miriam overly cheerful. 'All good. You?'

After the call, Evelyn spoke to Harold. 'Miriam sounded upset, as if something was wrong.'

Harold held his wife close. 'You always worry, darling. I'm sure she's fine.'

The only person who really understood was Mehreen. She and Miriam kept in touch throughout the many days and nights that followed, carrying each other through.

They reacted in different ways. Miriam felt sick and anxious, unable to concentrate on anything. Chris was quiet but tried to carry on with life as usual, insisting on regular mealtimes, despite Miriam having no interest in food.

But Daniel was angry. He was surprised at the rage within him, a torrent of fury that tumbled like a waterfall through his veins. Hannah had been offered a batmitzvah. She'd declined it and this was supposed to be his year, his summer, his first real chance to shine. Somehow Hannah always managed to twist the light back onto her. All the work he'd put in, the adulation: it was gone, as if it had never happened. It felt pointless. Why had he even bothered in the first place?

And there was another thing. He and Hannah each had savings jars in their bedrooms. Sometimes the family gave them money for treats or at Chanukah. Morris would sometimes slip them some coins. Daniel's had been emptied and so had Hannah's. How dare she? What gave her the right to do that? It was stealing.

Also, she'd been using The Laurel House for her and Taj whereas it had always been hers and Daniel's. He felt shoved aside, fed up. He'd never felt such fury before (even when a few kids at school had made silly anti-Jewish comments) and he didn't like what Hannah's behaviour was making him feel. She brought out the worst in him. She made him resentful. He looked in the mirror and didn't like what he saw. He thought he was a gentle, easy going boy. Now he saw a teenager full of venom, loathing the world.

Chris had made them a meal in the garden. Miriam, pale and black-ringed beneath her eyes, agreed to join them although she'd still no appetite. She held her phone in her hand, just in case.

‘I feel sick with worry,’ she said, accepting the plate of quiche and salad but unable even to look at it.

‘We know they’re safe,’ said Chris for what felt like the hundredth time.

‘But where are they? Where can they possibly be? I’m worried sick. I can’t take it any more.’

‘I think I know where they are,’ Daniel blurted out. His cheeks burned. He felt a mixture of shame at his exposing them and yet triumph. In a way, it was the most confused he’d ever felt. Revenge felt sweet but it also felt wrong.

‘What?’ shouted Miriam, springing up. ‘Why didn’t you say so before, Daniel?’

The truth was that he’d felt a certain weird loyalty to his sister but was also scared of her reaction when she found out that he’d been the snitch; then, he discovered that she’d taken his money, that was too much. The rage had been building uncontrollably within him. In a way, it was good to have Hannah out of the way so that the focus could be on him but it wasn’t working out that way. Mum was down and distracted and even his dad, who was always so mild, was hardly good company. They weren’t focussing on him, the way he’d hoped.

‘I’m not sure,’ he said tentatively, his heart thumping, ‘but they meet in the woods. I don’t know where it is exactly but they call it The Laurel House. I’ve heard Hannah talking about it on the phone to Taj.’

He blushed at his own half-truth. He couldn’t admit that it had been his and Hannah’s secret. It was a betrayal too far.

An hour later, Mehreen and Afzal, Hannah and Chris trampled in a line through the foliage as if volunteers in an organised search party. Brittle branches snapped beneath their feet. Overhead, the trees formed their own fans and canopies, where blackbirds and thrushes hid. The fanned leaves provided welcome shade from the blazing sun.

Jamil and Daniel stayed at the Steels' house, partly shocked by the events of the past few days, partly irritated by the drama. Who did their siblings think they were? Forbidden lovers in a great drama?

The woods covered a large expanse so it was hard to know where to look but it was Chris who seemed to have an instinct about it.

'There are lots of laurel trees over there,' he said. 'Let's try that.'

Then they heard voices and Miriam and Mehreen each lifted a side of the bush as if simultaneously opening curtains.

And there to their relief, they discovered Hannah and Taj.

Chris found the whole experience Shakespearean. The leafy bowers were reminiscent of *A Midsummer Night's Dream* and the revelation of the young couple reminded him of Ferdinand and Miranda, discovered playing chess: 'our dear-belov'd'.

There they were, cosy in the shelter that they'd created, living on the earth like pixies or wood-elves: Hannah in a pretty summer dress, Taj in t-shirt and shorts, a good looking couple, with a store of food and drink and books to sustain them. Some of their clothes were hanging from branches. For the rest of her life, Miriam would never forget how it felt to find them there, sparkling jewels in an emerald forest. It was magical. It was moving. It also felt sad, that they'd had to hide their love away: something to be ashamed of. They looked both safe and vulnerable.

Miriam rushed to hug Hannah, Mehreen to Taj, and they all made their way back to the Steels' house for an impromptu celebration, the mothers' arms around their children.

Chris made a barbecue, Afzal popped out to buy some vegetables and salads. They ate in the garden, the sun beaming approbation upon them.

Daniel thought to himself: when you are compliant and obedient in life, no-one congratulates or thanks you but when deviate and rebel, you get praise. It was all very confusing. He couldn't understand the way ahead, the world a strange place.

Jamil was quiet, trying to work out he felt about his brother's behaviour and wondering whether he would find love as strong as that one day.

Not noticing Daniel's thoughts, Miriam raised her glass happily in the air.

'To Hannah and Taj,' she said and everyone echoed her words.

Daniel twisted his face into a scowl. Why were Hannah and Taj being rewarded for running away, causing worry and lying?

Hannah saw this.

'Sorry about the money,' she whispered to him. 'You'll get it all back.'

The adults had already agreed: no scolding, no lectures, no punishment. Hannah and Taj were a couple and everyone would have to accept it, like it or not.

The following day Miriam rang Evelyn.

'Mum, I don't want an argument about it but I'm letting you know – and you can tell Ruth when you speak to her - that Hannah and Taj are together and that's it.'

Evelyn was taken aback by Miriam's strong tone.

'Of course, love. Why? Has anything happened?'

'Everything's alright now but there will be no further discussion about the issue. I won't be talking about it again. You'll just have to come to terms with it.'

'That fine, darling. We will.'

Miriam put the phone down. She never wanted to go through that ordeal again.

That shabbat, for the first time ever, Miriam and Ruth didn't ring each other.

Each sister found the void painful, but would not relent.

27

Miriam

Ruth had a plan. I didn't. I'm not sure which is better: life without a map or life with one. Ruth knew what she wanted: I didn't. I still don't. Neither of us has avoided disappointments and we've both had joy so maybe, in the end, it makes no difference.

We are diametric opposites. If we were plates of food, Ruth's would be ordered and arranged. Mine would be a messy mix. Luckily we aren't running a restaurant together. Can you imagine the rows?

I know that family's terribly important to me, the one I've come from and the one I've created. I sometimes think that Ruth feels that family, London and Judaism belong only to her. They don't. God is everywhere. He is there for us all.

I'm proud of being Jewish but I always felt that I wanted to be part of the world at large. I didn't want to live in a segregated community or a ghetto but join in with others whilst also retaining my own faith and identity. I admit, it's been harder than I thought it would be. It would have been easier to ditch my Judaism altogether, like Uncle Gerald has, but I can't. I value it too much.

For me, being Jewish is both joyful and painful. There's so much I love about it: family, music, warmth, camaraderie, humour, but there are difficult aspects to it too. To know that you are part of a race that has faced persecution and discrimination over centuries is hard and confusing. It isn't all just delightful. Antisemitism still exists. A woman I knew, Janine, a secretary at my previous school, converted to Judaism as she thought it would solve all her problems and bring her peace, but it didn't work out that way. Of course, some conversions go well, but she had too idealistic a vision of what Judaism is. She just saw the candles, wine and family. She didn't see the rest.

Daniel's bris was very hard. I knew that I had to go through with it but it was traumatic. I felt that Chris and I had a lot of tension over that. We were actually on the same side in finding it barbaric but I argued the opposite: many Jews, Muslims, and even members of the royal family have it done. It's supposed to be more hygienic. If Daniel marries a Jew, he will be expected to be circumcised. But I knew that in speaking to Chris, I was also trying to convince myself.

There wasn't a mohel in the area so we had to drive to London and back with a tiny baby. It was very stressful, as was seeing his little bandage afterwards and knowing that we had caused him pain. And all because of my cowardice: all because I didn't have the courage to say that I don't agree with it and was not willing to have it done. I did it for the family, not for my son.

My parents have been my role models. My dad worked with mostly non-Jews in his factory, as does my mum in her tough inner city primary school; but they do live in a Jewish area, Goldwell Hill, which makes it easier. When you're part of a minority, it's easier to either stay in a closed community, separate from the rest of society or shed your identity totally, but of course I've done neither. I chose the hard path, a messy one: the one less trodden.

Firstly, it has been difficult not having many Jews around. I get on with people of all colours, religions and creeds but sometimes it's good to be with those who understand your humour, faith, culture, food, references. It's tiresome always being different, having to explain who you are. I have, thankfully, experienced little antisemitism but I've certainly experienced ignorance. A woman at work said to me once, 'I heard on the radio that it's your Day of Atonement tomorrow. I wish you a happy festival.' Another said, 'Is it true that Jews can't eat peas?' I think she was referring to the issue about legumes at Pesach. Why do people always think that the most important aspect of Judaism is the food? I think it's the least important. Judaism is about values, how we live, how we treat others, what we believe, not just about what we can and cannot eat.

Secondly, it's difficult getting what you need. I like having a challah on Fridays and lighting a yartzeit candle for my bubba and zaider but, in this area, you can't always get what you want. Even finding a barmitzvah card is impossible.

Thirdly, there's the guilt. I worry. I fret. I analyse too much. One of the worst things I ever read was that Jews who 'marry out' are helping to complete Hitler's work. To compare the horrific slaughter of six million Jews with the decision to marry the man I love is terrible but that statement has never left me.

Fourthly, there is the issue of continuity. I want to instil the same pride in Judaism in my kids that I have, but not by hiding them away from others (as if Judaism is a precious orchid that can't survive in the cold). Rather, I want them to live in the real world and still be proud of who they are. Why can't an Afro-Caribbean or a Hindu retain their identity if they are surrounded by white Christians? Isn't that their right?

I weep at xenophobia and racism and discrimination of all kinds. Am I naïve? Am I idealistic?

Something else I read: you are judged as a Jew by whether you have Jewish grandchildren. Will I have any? Will my grandchildren be proud of their heritage? I don't know if Hannah will stay with Taj. I don't know if Daniel will marry someone Jewish. He hasn't shown any interest in girls yet. If they don't marry Jews and continue the line, my family will feel that I have failed. Can you imagine Ruth's reaction? But would I do the same again? I honestly don't know.

These are issues that Ruth never has to think about. I'm not saying that her life has been easy but at least she doesn't lie awake at night wrestling with these concerns.

Then there's the God debate. I think of myself as a reluctant atheist who's hoping that she's wrong; but I've genuinely never heard God's voice answer me although I've cried, called out and prayed. Ruth has a deep belief which I envy. She told me once that she felt she was being carried in the palm of God's hand and that she knew that He (how does she know God's gender?) would always look after her. How wonderful that must feel. Rabbi Woolf always says that although God is central to the lives of many Jews, it is much more about community, family and ideology than theistic belief. As he once said, 'You don't need to believe in God to be a good Jew but you do need to do what God says.' I like Woody Allen's comment: 'To you, I'm an atheist. To God, I'm the loyal opposition.'

What if I'm wrong? What if after death I arrive at who-knows-where (Judaism isn't very specific about Heaven, preferring, sensibly, to focus on the current life rather than on the afterlife) and God's there scolding me for not believing in him? Can you imagine the shame? The sense of failure?

I don't think it's only Jews who feel this. I've spoken to Christian and Muslim friends and they feel the same: the guilt! You're quite good but you're never good enough.

I don't know how I'd have managed without Mehreen. She faces exactly the same issues and dilemmas that I do. She wants her boys to be proud of their Muslim heritage and also be part of British society. She could have lived in a Muslim community, like her parents and siblings, but she chose not to. We understand each other. We listen to each other. We laugh together. We've also cried together.

In some ways it's harder for her than for me. There's even more Islamophobia than there's antisemitism. The difference is that whereas we are white and look more or less the same as others, she and her family are noticeable by the colour of their skin. Every time there's a terrible so-called Islamic atrocity, she's worried that her children will be picked on, just as each time Israel is in the news, antisemitism in this country increases, many people confusing anti-Zionism with anti-Judaism.

Mehreen's sister and mother wear the hijab but Mehreen's chosen not to. She dresses in a western style for work but when she goes to the mosque, of course, she dresses modestly and covers her head.

When I see a mixed marriage, let's say between a Portuguese national and someone from Macau, I think, how fascinating, what a rich heritage those children will have. But to some, like Ruth, they would see potential problems for the future, looking for trouble. She would stay: stick to your own.

When I read Donne's words

> No man is an island entire of itself.
> Every man is a piece of the continent,
> A part of the main….
> Any man's death diminishes me,
> Because I am involved in mankind,
> And therefore never send to know for whom the bell tolls;
> It tolls for thee.

I choke up. I'm moved to tears because that is exactly how I feel. I don't want anyone of any colour or race to suffer. I want to be a part of the world, the whole world in all its glory.

Look where division and segregation have got us. Northern Ireland. The Middle East. I do understand Gerald wanting nothing to do with it.

I was very proud of Daniel at his barmitzvah. He managed it with dignity and poise but it was important that he chose to do it himself and not because he was obliged to. Ruth took control of it all, as she tends to. She really is the older, bossy sister and I felt, as I always do, that she's always number one and that I'm always number two.

When I first realised what was going on between Hannah and Taj, I admit I was shocked. Then I felt torn. On the one hand, a Muslim boy and a Jewish girl is asking for trouble. I immediately thought of the reactions of others: Mum, Ruth, Ida, Gretel, society at large. But then another part of me thought: good. Break those barriers down. Knock away those divisions. The more we mix, the more we integrate, the better it will be. We will dispel ignorance.

Or will we just increase prejudice?

Who knows?

As I said before, I'm confused about religion.

No wonder my children are.

Recipe: kneidlach and dumplings

Kneidlach

Mix matzah meal, eggs, salt and pepper in a bowl.

Shape into balls.

Boil in water until they puff up.

Say the Shema while you wait.

Serve in chicken soup.

Dumplings

The same as above but use suet and flour instead of matzah meal.

While they boil, say The Lord's Prayer.

Serve in an Irish stew.

After both meals, go on a serious diet.

28

That healing feeling?

For several weeks, there was no contact between Miriam and Ruth. When Ruth and her family returned from Israel, there was usually a phone call and a catch-up but it didn't happen on this occasion. And after that first time of not ringing each other on shabbat, the barrier remained. It felt hard to break the silence. Each experienced the froideur differently: for Ruth, it felt like the culmination of years or disagreement and tension and somehow inevitable, as if she'd been waiting for it to happen. She'd always assumed that one day they'd break away from each other, their values, their attitudes to Judaism and life, irreconcilable. Sad though it was, she expected and accepted it. The thin string connecting them was eventually bound to fray and break.

But for Miriam, it was more painful than that. It just exemplified another rift between her and her roots, always feeling that she was being pushed out and ostracised. Ruth wouldn't really lose out if they never spoke again but for Miriam, it would sever her Jewish ties irrevocably. In the early hours of the morning, lying awake in the dark, she even wondered whether it was all a ruse, an excuse, to oust her from the family and community, something that Ruth may have been planning for years, but in the light of day, that seemed ridiculous.

Inevitably, Evelyn heard about the rift between her daughters and was distraught.

'The girls have had a falling out,' she told Harold one summer evening as they worked in the garden together. There were lettuces and carrots to pull out of the ground; everything needed watering.

Harold looked up. 'What now?'

‘Miriam and Ruth. They’re not speaking.’

‘Good,’ he said, unravelling the hose. ‘Maybe we can all have some peace and quiet.’

‘Don’t be silly, Harry. It can’t go on like this. It has to be resolved.’

Harold continued tending to the garden. He could understand why his father-in-law buried himself in nature. Since his retirement, he’d felt relieved not to be at work any longer but he still experienced stress. His chest often felt tight and the medication after his heart attack wasn’t as effective as he’d hoped it would be. There always seemed to be something to worry about: the boys’ barmitzvah; Ida hadn’t been that well; Morris had been quite low; Evelyn found a lump on her breast that luckily turned out to be benign.

And now this tsores with the girls.

‘Honestly, the kids at school are more mature. I’ll have to speak to them,’ which Evelyn did.

She phoned Ruth first: more level-headed, less emotional and dramatic.

They agreed to meet for coffee in a Jewish deli where they served great cheesecake.

‘I’m so sad about your rift with Miriam,’ she said to her daughter. The smartly-dressed woman opposite her had short, well-cut hair and wore a tailored navy trouser-suit.

‘What can I do, Mum? Miriam won’t shift. I’m fed up with her wanting everything her way. I’m tired of her saying she wants to be Jewish but then almost deliberately going against it. She needs to decide how she lives. Either she’s committed to it or she isn’t. It isn’t a game which you play some days and not others. At least Gerald’s consistent although I don’t agree with him. He doesn’t waver.’

Evelyn sipped her coffee quietly. She'd always tried not to take sides with her daughters or say anything which that be quoted back in a moment of rage. She felt that she was balanced precariously between them, not always a comfortable place to be.

'We can't change people, Ruth. Miriam has her own ideology and beliefs and we have to allow her to have those.'

'You're sounding very tolerant, Mum, but I know, deep down, you're not happy about it. Yet you always take her side.'

The phone call to Miriam was no easier.

'Darling, you have to understand Ruth's point of view.'

'Do I, Mum? Why?'

'Because she's allowed her opinion.'

'Is she? About my children? I don't interfere with hers.'

'I know but we are family -'

'It's my daughter, not hers.'

'Yes but Ruth's the older sister, protective of you.'

'The problem, Mum, is that you always take her side.'

Evelyn tried to focus on her parents (was Gretel getting dementia?), Harold (he was getting a worrying amount of chest pain lately), Morris (he was a bit blue) and Ida (she hadn't been well) while enjoying the summer, but the feud between her daughters was taking its toll. She'd dealt, in her life, with stress at work and in her family but this hurt her more than anything, even Gerald's rejection of her beliefs. If her daughters couldn't get on, it was the end of their family life: no shabbat meals, chagim at their homes, coming together for celebrations and events. And what would happen to the wonderful bond between the first cousins?

It broke her heart and put further strain on Harold's. What was supposed to be his peaceful retirement after a lifetime of work in a job he hadn't wanted, had become the opposite. Evelyn went on and on about the feud. Frankly, if he couldn't be on his fantasy island (palm trees, white sand) he'd rather be back at work. His wife used to talk about politics, Jewish issues and books, now spoke about nothing except the crack in her family and how to heal it.

One night, the incessant monologues continued in bed. Harold lay on his back, his stomach swollen. Evelyn had cooked an especially terrible chicken dish that night, experimenting with pickled gherkins in the sauce and it was so ghastly that Harold had had to cool his burning insides with too many scoops of vanilla ice-cream. Now it was all repeating on him in one hideous episode, as were Evelyn's words.

'It's terrible. The family that we've worked so hard to raise is over. We've failed, Harry. We've not been able to unite them. It's destroyed me.'

Harold could feel his heart pounding, his chest tightening and his stomach churning. He'd come out in a sweat and his face was boiling. In the darkness, the room spun, the curtains seeming to fall and the floor rise.

'To think of the sacrifices that we've made, all that we've done for them and this is how it turns out: a broken family who can't even bear to be in the same room as each other.'

Harold felt ill, bile filing his stomach and mouth.

'Evelyn,' he cried out in desperation. 'Call an ambulance. Now!'

29

Israel

When you hear the kinds of horrific details that I do, day after day, it's very hard to cling onto your own sanity. It's also very difficult not to be cynical about people.

I listen to those who've been damaged by the greed, violence, hatred and brutality of others and I witness the effect that it's had. Yes, medication and therapy can be helpful but I know that people cannot be wholly saved from the past. In that sense, I'm a fraud as I claim that I can help them when I know that what I can offer is actually rather limited.

When I was a young psychiatrist, I was less affected by what I heard. Maybe I had more conviction that I could help but also I was naïve and idealistic about it. Now I've heard so much that it's hard to cope with at times. I'm less resilient now than I used to be, as if my body and armour are worn.

Because I'm a Jewish psychiatrist, quite a few of my clients are Jewish. They've often lost family members in the Holocaust or have suffered horrific antisemitism. It's hard to listen to them and the danger is that psychiatrists can become immune or hardened to what they hear. That is our self-protection so we nod and show compassion but we are faking to some extent, like an actor pretending to cry or die on stage. He's using a code, a language, a series of symbols for what he's really feeling and we're the same. It's not that we don't care but we're preventing ourselves from caring too much.

As a child growing up in a loving Jewish home, I thought that Judaism was wholly benign and delightful. There was an atmosphere of sweet wine, candles and singing; of women cuddling us to their ample breasts and of men touching us kindly on the shoulder, slipping us coins and smiling with their eyes. It always felt warm in our home.

It was a shock, later on, to learn that many people don't like the Jews. Hearing about the Holocaust was massive: the brutality, that horrific slaughtering of innocent people. I couldn't understand that this lovely warm religion could engender hatred in others. Even now, although I can try to rationalise it, I cannot understand it. 'Man's inhumanity to man' might be everywhere but it makes no sense.

Gretel, my wife, is a dear lady but I have found her worrying and moaning over the years rather trivial. Because she hasn't heard what I have, she's often superficial. She cares more about the surface than the substance. She can be rather silly: which tablecloth should she use? Are the avocadoes ripe enough? Should she have her hair dyed or let it grow grey? These are foolish concerns when others have endured torture, rape, abuse, neglect.

She's deteriorated of late, not only in looks - she used to be so pretty, dark shiny eyes, high cheekbones - but also in her behaviour. She repeats herself and gets confused about dates. I've treated many patients with dementia so I'm familiar with the symptoms and know what lies ahead. I dread it. She looks like an old, wrinkled lady now and behaves like one too.

Officially I've retired but I still keep some private patients, mainly to get me out of the house. I stay out longer than I need to, have some coffee on the way home, take my time. I'm not ready to be at home all day long, listening to Gretel's concerns.

Gretel has found our son Morris's homosexuality hard to bear. We've talked endlessly about it - or she has while I've listened – legs crossed, head to one side, my professional pose; but she can't come to terms with it. She wouldn't mind others being gay, but not her son. She loves him but she has rather a rigid notion of how life should be: marriage, family, grandchildren. Maybe if he was happy, she'd be more at peace but she knows he isn't. All those jokes and bluffing. It is so clear that they are his cloak.

So Gretel worries about him but she also worries about Evelyn and her family: Miriam's gap year; Ruth's miscarriages; Simon's business having a bad spell, David's shyness; Harold's heart attack; Hannah's boyfriend; and on it goes.

As for Gerald! Gretel simply can't accept his rejection of religion. She's quite solipsistic in that sense: she can't see others' points of view. She wouldn't make a good psychiatrist, as she wants everyone to share her views and can't understand why they don't. If she isn't talking about Morris, it's Gerald. She wanted straight, married, Jewish sons who went to shul and adhered to her notion of what life should be. It doesn't always work out like that. She sees other families where the sons have toed the line and she wonders why her boys haven't. It doesn't bother me (I don't see life as an instruction manual) and I can't see why it bothers her so. She's an intelligent woman but instead of developing her mind, she goes on about the same issues. She's a stuck record and, frankly, it's wearing. What can I do about it? There's such a thing as free will.

I do rather love my vegetables. They have no consciousness. They do not speak or moan, analyse or complain. They are just what they are. I love the yellow star flowers on the courgettes; the velvety aubergines and the substantial marrows; the peas and beans that climb and curl around poles; tomatoes blushing at their own ripeness. I talk to them and nurture them. They grow huge. They benefit from my care in a visible, tangible way – more responsive than some of my patients.

At Pesach, everyone now looks forward to my horseradish, which I grow specially each year. It is quite pungent and can make the eyes water. I don't mean to inflict pain on others but then again I like the immediacy. In a profession where I can't always see results as quickly or clearly as I would like, this is pleasing.

Eat it. See the reaction.

Recipe: Chicken soup (Jewish penicillin)

Put a chicken in a pot with onions, carrots, leeks and celery.

Cover with water and a lid and boil for three days.

If you are frum, don't add butter. If you aren't frum, do.

Serve in a bowl.

Watch the meat fall off the bone, your family's ailments fade away and everyone's mood improve.

30

New year, old feuds

What Miriam had always loved about Rosh Hashanah was the newness, the freshness of it all. It was like another chance, another opportunity. If the past year had been tough, this one could undoubtedly be better. It was a festival of optimism, of looking ahead.

Each year, Evelyn covered the table with a white cloth, linen napkins to match, and there was always a vase of white roses at the centre, their buds tight and neat. A round challah would be flanked by candles and wine and there was sliced apple ready to dip into honey, a symbolic hope that the coming days would be sweet.

This year, however, there was no Rosh Hashanah meal. Harold was still in hospital, after his second heart attack, and Evelyn went to see him each day after work.

Miriam and Ruth, still not talking, kept in touch with their mum and visited their dad separately. Gradually, over time, he started regaining his colour, his energy and his sense of fun.

When Miriam went to him, she smuggled in pickled herring and gherkins inside her handbag.

'But Dad, when you come home, you'll really have to watch your diet.'

'Don't tell me. You sound like my consultant. I might have to give up your mother's cooking. What a tragedy. How sad.' And he winked at his daughter.

Ruth, on her visits, was just as concerned.

'Dad, you're so important to us. You'll need to be more careful with exercise and diet.'

'I know,' said Harold, resignedly. 'I'll eat like a rabbit from now on. Celery for breakfast and lettuce for lunch.' He twitched his nose.

Neither daughter mentioned the stress they'd caused him. To avoid saying it might mean that it had never happened. Harold didn't allude to it, always evading conflict when he could.

Evelyn wasn't as forgiving, however.

She wrote her girls a letter:

My darling daughters,

Rosh Hashanah is usually one of my favourite chagim when, as you know, we all come together for a lovely family occasion.

Not this year.

With your father in hospital, my attention's on him, visiting him each day. Because Daddy isn't here, I won't host our usual meal. It doesn't feel right without him but that's not the only reason.

I'm not happy with the way that you've both behaved. We brought you up to be kind and tolerant and you haven't, sadly, displayed these qualities to each other.

Yes, you have chosen different paths in life but that shouldn't mean that you have to turn against each other. Jews have enough problems with others without us falling out amongst ourselves.

You've both been stubborn and obstinate, refusing to admit wrongdoing or apologise.

You're setting a bad example for your children, who adore each other, and you've caused Daddy and me terrible pain.

I'm disappointed.

I've been to see Rabbi Woolf who has said that a period of time apart and reflection may be helpful, especially at this time of year. He's also said that he'd be happy to meet you together if you like.

I wish you and your families shanah tovah.

Even though I'm hurt, I love you always,

Your unhappy Mum

Both women read the letter with tears in their eyes and shame in their hearts – but they still didn't relent. Ruth sent her mum white flowers, while and Miriam sent a box of pampering treats, herbal soap, shampoo, two soft flannels.

Rosh Hashanah came. There was a sombre mood.

Ruth and Simon took their kids to shul on the day and then to his parents for a meal. It was hard for Masha to manage it all, with Joel to look after, but they made a lovely spread and Adam led the prayers.

In the car on the way home, the kids complained.

'We like it more when we go to our other bubbe and zaider's,' said Abby, unusually moany.

'I miss seeing Daniel,' said David, quietly.

'Why aren't we with our cousins as usual?' asked Leah.

'It didn't work out this year, with zaider in hospital,' said Ruth, uncomfortable at her own half-truth.

'Maybe next year,' said Simon, supporting his wife.

Ruth was quiet. Miriam had caused her so much pain over the years with her implied criticism; she'd wondered if it might be easier not to see her again. But it was obvious now that their rift would hurt so many others – and her. But how did they heal it? Who would apologise first?

Miriam spent the day alone. When the children were younger, she'd insisted that they stayed home from school but now that they weren't going to London, it didn't seem necessary. She still had the day off as agreed with the school (although Fletcher scowled at her the day before) and, even though he offered to stay with her, she insisted that Chris should go to work.

The beauty of the weather felt incongruous with her mood. A blue September sky stretched itself across her garden, an oasis. Coffee in her hand, she walked slowly around, admiring the vegetables Chris had grown: lettuces green and frilly; courgettes sturdy and firm and the last of the strawberries, clinging resolutely on. She felt humbled and quiet.

Yes, she and Ruth had taken very different paths, but their rift was causing pain to her and her children. It may even have triggered her dad's heart attack. Miriam admitted to herself that she was jealous of Ruth, that although in some ways she didn't want her life, in other ways she did.

She sat in the gentle sun and read the prayerbook, the Rosh Hashanah evening and following morning services, the mediations too, and one line stood out to her, Chasidic words:

'People cannot find redemption until they see the flaws in their souls and try to efface them. We can be redeemed only to the extent to which we see ourselves.'

She cried, she smiled. It was as if years of pain and questioning had led her to this point.

'Lord,' she called out, 'help us move forward and please let my daddy live.'

By the time that Chris and the kids came home that evening, Miriam had prepared a lovely meal. She'd laid a white tablecloth as her mum always did and made salmon and vegetables. She kept the prayers to the minimum and they ate together, feeling united but also strange.

Israel and Gretel ate ready-made food as Gretel was finding it harder to co-ordinate the components of their meals. Israel said a few prayers and then he went down to tend his plants while Gretel watched his solid frame from the large window, bending to his task, his back turned to her.

Ida was alone. A family from the shul had kindly invited her for first night but she declined. She didn't always want to be the spare wheel at the party and besides, she was too upset about her brother. She couldn't consider life without Harold – his kindness, his care. She'd been to see him in hospital and he'd looked terrible: pasty, bloated. She feared the worst. It kept her awake at night.

Morris ordered a takeaway. He spent the evening quietly, drinking whisky. He recalled a few jokes in his head -

So…my friend Esther is so religious that after she sleeps with the butcher, she always waits four hours before sleeping with the milkman - but there was no-one to tell them to so he kept silent. Without an audience, they didn't seem as funny.

Evelyn went to see Harold in hospital and recited prayers with him. Then she went home. Several families had invited her for dinner but she'd politely refused. If she couldn't have her own family with her, she'd rather be alone.

She looked at the dining room where the table had been folded away. There was no warmth, no laughter. The candles weren't lit. The wine was unopened. The house wasn't filled with the smell of dinner cooking. She thought of the people usually there: Morris with his inappropriate jokes; Ida scowling; the children giggling; Miriam and Chris; Ruth and Simon, and her dear Harold at the head of the table, pretending it was all too noisy and chaotic for him but secretly loving it. She remembered all the gatherings when they were children and the laughter and the joy.

She made herself a sandwich with some leftover chicken and sat alone in the living room, looking at the framed photos of her family: her wedding, her parents' wedding and her in-laws too; a lovely one of Ruth with her family in Jerusalem; another of Miriam and her family in a French sunflower field; a sweet one of Ruth and Miriam as children in their garden, on their bikes; the girls' batmitzvahs.

Where had she and Harold gone wrong? Had they been too lenient or too firm? Should they stand back or take more action? What could they do? Was it the end of their family life?

She bit into her sandwich but it stuck in her throat.

She wept.

Never before had she felt such pain.

31

Yom Kippur: no cholent but a time to repent

The eight days between Rosh Hashanah and Yom Kippur lagged. The previously sunny days became greyer, as if the sky was reclothing itself for the shift from celebration to reflection; outward joy to sombre introspection.

Evelyn focused on her work, only taking off her two allocated days and working doubly hard the rest of the time there. It was a hectic period at school with new assessments being trialled and, as the Deputy Head, she had to ensure the smooth running of this process. There had also been several staff with illness so she had to arrange cover for them.

Each day she left school and headed straight to the hospital.

After ten days, Harold was allowed home. Somehow, his discharge seemed appropriately timed for this period, poised between the joy of new year and the melancholy of Yom Kippur. She was thrilled to see him home again but this happiness was tinged with caution.

'He will need to rest and take it easy,' said the doctor, 'and there's significant weight to be lost.'

He looked sternly over his glasses.

'I hear you loud and clear, doctor,' said Harold, accepting his rebuke. 'Thank you for everything.'

It felt strange to Harold, returning home. The absence seemed much longer than ten days. Being in hospital was like being in another universe: the smell, the sheets, the food, so different from the home he knew and loved.

Being away had also allowed him to separate himself from what else was always going on. It felt like another country.

'I assume the girls are still being stubborn and not communicating?' he said to Evelyn.

She nodded. She regretted the stress she'd put on Harold (had she even triggered his heart attack?) and so had vowed to be more reserved on the issue.

'They're adults,' she said. 'They'll have to sort it out for themselves.'

She and Harold stayed at home for Yom Kippur. She fasted; he didn't, knowing that Judaism never asks people to endanger their health. Instead, he enjoyed the soup that Evelyn had made him to eat on his own.

They read and prayed, talked and reminisced.

'It's so good to have you home,' she said, 'my dear, dear Harry.'

Ruth and her family went to shul and they all fasted, apart from Abby who was too young to do so. They broke the fast with a meal at Simon's parents' home, once again lamenting the fact that they were missing their usual meal at the other bubbe and zaider's.

Miriam had another quiet day at home, fasting, reading the words of the prayerbook which took on an extra significance this time, especially in the confession:

'We were obstinate. We have perverted and quarrelled,'

And she read aloud: 'Our God and God of our fathers, have mercy on us, and pardon all our sins; grant atonement for all our iniquities, forgiveness for all our transgressions.'

Hundreds of miles away, Ruth read the same words and both women felt ashamed.

Maybe this was why, when the rabbi's secretary contacted them after Yom Kippur, to offer them a joint meeting with the rabbi, they both agreed.

It felt strange to the sisters as they entered Rabbi Woolf's study, avoiding each other's eyes. He welcomed them and they both sat down.

'Miriam, Ruth,' he began, 'I'm going to tell you a story. A rowing couple, accompanied by a chaperone friend, went to see the rabbi to ask for a divorce. "Fine," said the rabbi, and he asked the woman. "Why do you want a divorce?" and she said, "Because my husband is selfish and lazy." "You're right," said the rabbi. And he asked the man, "Why do you want a divorce?" And the man replied, "Because my wife is moody and cold." "You're right," said the rabbi.

The chaperone friend was confused. "Sorry, rabbi. I don't understand. First you said that the wife was right. Then you said that the husband was right."

"You're right," said the rabbi.'

'Miriam and Ruth, you are both right but you are also both wrong. Your parents are two of the kindest people whom I have ever had the pleasure to meet. They are good, generous, selfless: everything that Jews ought to be. You are causing them terrible pain.'

The two women looked down. Miriam raked her fingers through her hair. Ruth fiddled with the buttons on her jacket.

'So you've chosen different paths in life. That's fine but there's no need to judge or condemn each other. You are family. I want to witness in you both more of what your parents have taught you: tolerance, compassion and respect.'

Feeling like two naughty children who have been reprimanded by the head, they thanked the rabbi and left.

Outside the shul, Miriam and Ruth hugged each other before they spoke.

'I'm sorry, Mims,' said Ruth.

'I'm sorry, too, Ruthie.'

They drank coffee at a small place where the cakes stood proudly in a glass cabinet.

'We must never fall out again,' said Ruth, and Miriam agreed.

'We've made different choices but that's fine. As the rabbi says, it doesn't mean that we can't be close.'

They talked about their work, about their children, but both sisters could feel themselves treading carefully, as if on broken glass. As they veered towards awkward subjects they drew back, as if those topics had electric wire around them. By the time they parted company, Ruth to walk home and Miriam to the train station, they knew that something was better. Something had healed. They had put family harmony first.

But something had also been irrevocably lost, like a jigsaw accepting that some pieces were missing and would never be found.

Recipe: delicious knishes

Use any pastry you like: strudel dough, unsweetened biscuit dough or a flaky dough.

Cut into circles.

Fill with potato, chicken or cheese.

Fold and bake.

When they're cool, enjoy your delicious knishes and make your wishes.

Wipe your mouth and give your partner kishes.

32

Gretel

Life doesn't always work out as easily as you might expect.

Israel and I met at the hospital in Goldwell Hill. He was training to be a doctor, then a psychiatrist and I was a secretary. Some women want their own careers and are ambitious. That's fine. I never was. What's mattered more than anything is to have a happy family life. When you see families destroyed by the Shoah, then you know how precious those relationships are and want to hold your loved ones close.

Israel was tall, handsome and serious. He seemed rooted, anchored, not only in his work but physically, the way he stood, with poise and stillness, showing that he was reliable. We liked each other straight away but there's never been a great passion there. We aren't soulmates. We're people who have made a home together and have similar values and beliefs. We've been good parents, I think.

From a young age, Morris was different from the other boys. I could see it. He didn't want to climb trees and kick a ball around. He was sensitive and clever but always overweight. He found it hard to settle at school and to make friends. I used to say all this to Israel but he never took much interest. It hurt me that he was more interested in his clients – and vegetables – then he was in his son or his wife.

So I tried to support Morris the best I could. He became more confident when he got a book of jokes as a gift and then he became the joke-teller. I find him very funny. His timing is excellent, pausing for effect and delivering in a slightly dry monotone. Some of the jokes are a bit racy for my liking but I do still laugh. I don't know how he remembers them all.

His homosexuality is very hard for me. The Bible doesn't condone it and nor, to be honest, do I. I think that God created men and women, beginning with Adam and Eve, so that they could procreate. But of course I love my son. I don't know if he's lonely. He never says he is so I assume he's alright. I think he's quite happy. Surely he wouldn't tell so many jokes if he were sad.

Then there's Gerald. He was always a strong-willed child and had his own opinions on everything. His school reports often commented on this. He wasn't always easy at home, quarrelling with us, pointing out why he disagreed. He wanted reasons for everything. If I said, 'You need to come to see your bubbe and zaider with us,' he'd ask why. 'Because they're family,' I'd answer. 'So what?' came the reply. 'They will still be family if I don't go to see them.'

When he told me, after his barmitzvah, that he wouldn't be going to shul again, it nearly destroyed me. It was such a shock. I couldn't understand it: he'd performed so well. The only way I could cope with it was by telling myself that it was just a phase, that he was being a stubborn adolescent and that he'd change his mind; but he never did. If anything his views have become more entrenched over time.

Gerald's wife Jenny isn't Jewish. She was brought up in a weird religious cult. She isn't very warm and neither are her children. I know them least of my four grandchildren. (Of course, Morris is childless.) As they won't be involved in anything Jewish it cuts so much out.

My sons, each in their own way, have unwittingly broken my heart.

Evelyn has, at least, led the kind of life I am more comfortable with. She was a much easier child, settling well and always popular. I like Harold although I think he lacks ambition. I also worry about his heart. He needs to lose weight and Evelyn should be firmer about it. Miriam and Ruth are lovely girls – so different from each other – but there again there have been issues. Miriam married out and her children aren't leading the kind of Jewish life I'd have liked. Ruth has a lovely husband, Simon, but they've had sad times with miscarriages and their son David, who lacks self-confidence.

I lie in bed worrying about my family. When you've devoted your life to them, you are so invested in and concerned for them. You feel their pain. You share their joy. I have some good women friends and am very involved in the shul, especially the charity committee. We raise money for good causes. I like arranging the flowers for weddings and barmitzvahs, often using blooms from our garden. Even there, Israel and I are apart: he's only interested in vegetables; me in flowers.

I haven't told anyone but I feel very lonely at times. I know that I've a lot to be grateful for: a beautiful house and garden; a husband with a good job; time to myself; but when I tell Israel about my day, he doesn't really listen. That hurts me: he focuses on strangers but not his own wife. Maybe I should pay him. Maybe then he'd listen. I wish he would retire (he's the oldest psychiatrist in the team and well passed retirement age) but he won't stop working. I suppose it makes him feel worthwhile. That must be the reason.

We've slept in separate beds for years. We don't undress in front of each other. We don't touch and cuddle any more. It's been so long now that it would feel strange to do so. If we watch a film with intimate scenes, we feel embarrassed. I wish Israel would wrap his long, strong arms around me and kiss my hair, but he never does. When I see his elegant tall figure bend down close to inspect a courgette flower or stroke the leaves of an aubergine, I feel sad that he never lavishes any attention on me. It is ridiculous to feel jealous of a vegetable, but I do.

I don't know if Israel still loves me. I dare not ask. I don't know if I love him anymore but I care for him. Maybe marriage changes over the years. I didn't think when we first married that I would ever feel isolated. I thought that I'd have a companion for life but although Israel's still here, I don't feel his presence. He's both present and absent at the same time.

We've never talked about separation or divorce. That's out of the question. I think couples these days don't work hard enough at their marriages. Relationships are hard. You have to keep going, not give up. Evelyn's very good and often invites us to events but we rarely go. Israel is always back late from work or too tired to go out. I could go on my own but I don't feel that's right. I should be with my husband. Also, I need more rest as I get older and the family dos are often noisy and go on until late.

My memory's not as good as it used to be and I get muddled. Israel says, 'Do you remember that day…?' and I don't. I forget the names of actors, the titles of books, films.

I may not be very academic but I think a lot. I wonder what life is about. I pray to God. I call out to Him. He tells me that I am good and that I should carry on. So that is what I do. I try to be kind and to be the best person that I can.

Every day I read the meditation in the prayerbook and try to live by it: 'May the words of my mouth and the meditation of my heart be acceptable to you, O God, my Rock and my Redeemer.'

Amen.

33

Chanukah and Christmas again

Once again, they gathered at Harold and Evelyn's house.

In the time since their healing of the sisterly rift, Ruth and Miriam had kept in touch as usual, consulting over dates for family events, asking after each others' children but their conversation was now polite and slightly distant. Both felt, privately, that something had shifted, like moving sand and the treasure inside it had been lost forever. But to sacrifice family life and the happiness of others was too much to bear. On that, they were agreed.

In the centre of the table there was the lit chanukiah – it was the fifth day – standing firm in a sea of chocolate coins and sweets. Evelyn had made latkes (Harold was only allowed one) and there were doughnuts and biscuits, no oiliness spared.

At the top of the table, a slightly slimmer Harold sat quietly, surveying his family. Evelyn was beside him, holding his hand. Ida saw them and missed her husband, even after all these years. Morris, next to her, as he always seemed to be, was pleased to have an audience again:

'So…Rebecca and Rachel meet in the street. "How are you, Rebecca?" asks Rachel. "Fine thank you," answers Rebecca. "My husband's work's going well, my daughter's engaged and my son's just got a promotion." "Great," says Rachel, "but you know, Rebecca, we meet in the street. I ask you how you are and you tell me. But you never ask me how I am." "I'm so sorry," says Rebecca. How rude of me. So how are you?" "Ach," says Rachel. "Don't ask." '

Miriam and Ruth laughed. Evelyn smiled politely: she'd heard the joke a hundred times before.

Miriam looked down to the bottom of the table where the cousins sat together, laughing and talking. Hannah looked much happier now that the family had accepted Taj. She was enjoying her last year at school and looking forward to taking a gap year before going to university to read History. She and Taj were applying to the same places: him to read Politics. Here they sat, side by side, feeling less awkward as time went on.

Daniel looked happier too. He was enjoying Year Nine at school and starting to think about which GCSEs to take. He was veering much more towards the sciences (even though he was also good at English and creative writing) distinguishing himself from Hannah. It reminded her of Ruth and herself, making different choices, marking out their territories and their lives.

Leah and Abby were as bubbly as ever, the smaller girl with sweet gaps in her mouth where her milk teeth had fallen out. David looked more content too. Managing the barmitzvah with Daniel had clearly boosted his self-confidence and everyone (other than Ida) seemed positive - she never changed. Even when she was showing snaps of her new grandchild, Jael, in Israel, she didn't smile.

And there was Chris, lanky and quiet, listening, reflective, taking it all in and demanding nothing back.

The conversation was as busy and buzzy as always:

'How's business, Simon?'

'You've definitely lost weight, Harold.'

'Really: you think so?'

'I like your top. Is it new?'

'It was in the summer sale.'

'I see they're making a new series of *Shitsel.*'

'Oh, I finished the Howard Jacobson. It was wonderful. You want to borrow it?'

'Did you hear? Ariel's expecting twins.'

'Twins? You hair looks nice. Did you have it cut?'

'And coloured. Just the roots.'

But when Harold raised his glass to thank Evelyn for the delicious meal (they were on coffee and chocolates by now) and everyone said, 'L'chaim!' Miriam took her chance, as there was a slight gap to say:

'I want to raise as well, a toast to Chris; or should I say Professor Chris Steel?'

She looked proud; her husband looked shy.

'Oh Chris, that's amazing news. Mazal tov.'

'What? When?'

'He's been given a personal chair from this year as his new book's coming out and he has been commissioned to write another one.'

There were cheers; there was applause.

Chris reddened, unused to being the centre of everyone's gaze.

Miriam had caught Ruth's eye over dinner. The slight discomfort between them was slowly healing. Recovery always took time but tentatively, carefully they smiled at each other. No-one ever wanted a repeat of the awful Rosh Hashanah and Yom Kippur when the family splintered.

Evelyn suddenly looked older, paler, as if the events of the past year had taken their toll on her. Individually, each daughter felt guilty for the pain caused.

'I have news too,' said Harold. Everyone looked up. 'The rabbi has challenged me to a sponsored diet competition. We'll raise money for charity – him for the shul, me for the British Heart Foundation – and see who can lose more.'

More applause, more cheers.

That year, the festivals didn't overlap and Chanukah was over before Christmas had begun, allowing it some space of its own.

Back in their home, on Christmas Day, Miriam looked at the tree less resentfully than the year before. It seemed to matter less to Hannah now that she was with Taj. Daniel was happy with the decorations, but barmitzvahed, he'd decided that he would spend more time at Aunty Ruth's house, he and David closer than ever. Miriam had mixed feelings about this: in a way, she was pleased that he was proud of being Jewish, but the fact that he wanted to spend more time with Ruth and her family also hurt her. It was yet another example of Ruth having won. Miriam worried that her sister would steal Daniel's affections.

As usual, they went to Ian and Maureen for Christmas Day lunch, staggering home several hours, and pounds, heavier. Maureen's Christmas pudding had seemed even denser than usual, as if she had filled it with wet sand.

School would be starting again soon.

They settled back into their home, pleased to have been away; happy to return.

Miriam looked around her at the washing waiting to be folded, the mess, the chaos, the books haphazardly on the shelves, plants that she'd forgotten to water, and she saw that it was mayhem, a jumble, mixed,

Behind the tree, on the dresser, the Chanukiah sat, already used that year, melted wax on its front, humbled.

Amongst the Seasons' Greetings cards there was one from Lucas: 'Thank you Miss for being my best teecher ever.'

And that shabbat the sisters resumed their weekly call with civility if not affection:

'Shabbat shalom, Ruthie.'

'Shabbat shalom, Mims.'

Harold's recipe for a happy family life

Be tolerant.

Be kind.

Forgive mistakes.

Sing a lot.

Eat even more.

Tell jokes.

Dance.

Hug.

Never stop loving.

Warning

This novel is full of raw chicken.

This is a comic device.

Always make sure that your chicken is well cooked.

Evelyn's is not.

Don't try this at home.

Spare Jokes for Morris

Morris has some extra jokes for which there wasn't room in the book. He'd like to share them with you.

So… a rabbi calls in his friend, another rabbi, for advice on getting rid of the mice in his shul. 'It's easy,' advises the second one. 'Put a yarmulke on each one, barmitzvah them and you'll never see them again.'

So….two women are sitting on a park bench. 'Oh ya yoy!' says one.

'I thought we agreed not to talk about the children,' says the other.

So… Hymie is downbeat. He says to Rebecca, 'I can't remember the last time you enjoyed sex.'

'Why would you?' she says. 'You weren't there.'

So….Rebecca, Hymie's wife, advises her niece. 'When you look for a husband there are five points to remember. 1. He must be helpful in the house. 2. He must earn well. 3. He must spoil you. 4. He must make you laugh. 5. These four men mustn't know each other.'

So…'You know,' says Rebecca to Hymie, 'when we were younger, you used to nibble my ear.'

Hymie gets out of bed.

'Where are you going?' she asks.

'To get my teeth.'

So…a Jewish woman says to her rabbi. 'I love Hymie and I love Moishe. Who will be the lucky one?'

'Marry Moishe,' says the rabbi. 'Hymie will be the lucky one.'

So…Hymie says to Rebecca. 'Money's tight. If only you would cook, we could sack the housekeeper.'

'If only you could make love,' she says, 'we could sack the gardener.'

So…Hymie is on his deathbed.

'Are all the family here?' he asks.

'Yes,' is the reply.

'Then who's minding the shop?'

So…Hymie is at the grocers.

'How much are those?

'Two for a pound.'

'How much is just one?

'Seventy five pence.'

'I'll have the other one.'

So…Rebecca says to Hymie, 'Come upstairs and make love to me.'

'I can do one or the other,' he says. 'Not both.'

So…one year Hymie gives his wife a burial plot for her birthday. The next year he gives her nothing.

Rebecca is hurt.

'Why didn't you get me anything?' she asks.

'Well,' he replies. 'Why should I give you a present? You didn't use the one I gave you last time.'

So…when Hymie and Moishe were 55, they went to eat at Ryan's because the food was good.

When they were 65, they went there because they had wheelchair access.

When they were 75, they went there because they hadn't been there before.

So…the Italian says, 'I'm tired and thirsty. I must have wine.'

The Frenchman says, 'I'm tired and thirsty. I must have cognac.'

The Russian says, 'I'm tired and thirsty. I must have vodka.'

The German says, 'I'm tired and thirsty. I must have beer.'

The Mexican says, 'I'm tired and thirsty. I must have tequila.'

The Jew says, 'I'm tired and thirsty. I must have diabetes.'

So…Rebecca turns up, when summoned, for jury service.

But they send her home. She kept insisting *she* was guilty.

So…Moishe goes to see the psychiatrist.

'You know. Yesterday I had the strangest dream and I hope you could explain it to me. I was in bed with both my mother and mother-in-law.

Then I went downstairs and had coffee and toast for breakfast.'

'Toast and coffee?' says the psychiatrist. 'You call that breakfast?'

So…Hymie goes to the doctor.

'You're going to die.'

Moishe is stunned. 'I'd like a second opinion.'

'You're also ugly,' says the doctor.

So…Hymie says to Moishe.

'I'm thinking of divorcing my wife.'

'Why's that?' asked Moishe.

'She hasn't spoken to me for two months.'

'Think carefully about it,' says Moishe. 'Women like that are hard to find.'

So… Moishe says to Hymie.

'Guess what? I'm sleeping with a blonde, one of twins but I'm also sleeping with the other one.'

Hymie asks, 'How do you tell them apart?'

'It's easy,' replies Moishe. 'Her brother's got a moustache.'

So…Hymie calls over the waiter.

'Are you the waiter I first gave my order to?'

'Yes,' says the waiter. 'Why do you ask?'

'Because I was expecting a much older man by now.'

So…Hymie goes to the doctor.

'You know, no-one listens to me. I feel insignificant.'

'Next,' says the doctor.

So…Moishe tells Hymie.

'Guess what? I've got a new hearing aid. State of the art.'

'Great,' says Hymie. 'What make is it?'

'Twelve thirty,' replies Moishe.

So…Hymie goes to confession and tells the priest.

'I'm ninety years old and I have a twenty seven year old girlfriend.'

'That's great,' says the priest, 'but why are you telling me? I'm Catholic and you're Jewish.'

'Are you kidding?' says Hymie. 'I'm telling everyone!'

So…Hymie says to Rebecca, 'For our golden wedding anniversary, would you like a party?'

'No,' she says.

'A cruise?'

No.

'Then what do you want?'

'A divorce.'

'Gee, I wasn't thinking of spending that much.'

Bibliography

No research was undertaken for the writing of this novel.

To quote Ida, 'Why should I bother? Did you?'

Glossary

Afikomen: matzah hidden at Passover for a child to find

aliyah: moving to Israel

bagels: round rolls with holes in the middle

batmitzvah/barmitzvah: rite of passage into adulthood

bimah: platform in the synagogue

borsht: beetroot soup

bracha (pl. brachot): blessing

bris: circumcision

bubba: grandmother

Chad Gadya: a Passover song

challah: plaited loaf

Chanukah: festival of lights

chanukiah: nine hole candlestick

charoshet: nut and apple paste eaten at Passover

chatzilim: aubergine salad

cheder: Jewish Sunday school

cholent: meat and vegetable dish

chraine: beetroot horseradish

chremslach: matzah pudding

chuppah: wedding canopy

chutzpah: cheek, audacity

dreidls: spinning tops played with at Chanukah

d'var Torah: commentary on Torah passage

Eid: end of Ramadan

Elijah: prophet

falafel: chickpea balls

frum: religious

gefilte fish: cooked fish dish

gut shabbos: sabbath greeting

Haftorah: readings from the Jewish Bible

Haggadah: book for the service at Passover

halva: sweet made from honey

Hamantaschen: pastries eaten at Purim

Hassid: religious Jew

hijab: head covering worn by Muslim women

Hillel: one of the foremost rabbis in Judaism

humous: chickpea dip

kibbutz: community in Israel

kiddush: blessings sung after a service

kichlach: pastries

kippah (pl. kippot): skullcap worn by Jewish men

knishes: pastry parcels

kosher: food adhering to strict Jewish code

kneidluch: dumplings

kugel: pudding

latkes: potato cakes

L'Chaim: good health, cheers

lokshen: noodle or pasta pudding

Maccabi: Jewish youth group

Magen David: star of David

Ma Nishtana: song sung by the youngest person at Passover

Ma'otsur: song sung at Chanukah

Maror: bitter herbs

matzah: unleavened bread

Mazal tov: congratulations

menorah: same as a chanukiah

meshugge: crazy

mezuzah: religious text posted on door

mikveh: cleansing waters

mitzvah: good deed

mohel: carries out the circumcision

nachas: luck, good fortune

nudnik: nuisance

Oy Ya Yoy: an expression of despair

parashah: portion of Torah

Pesach: Passover

pupik: part of a chicken

Purim: festival of Esther

rabbi: religious leader of a synagogue

Ramadan: Muslim festival

Rosh Hashanah: Jewish new year

RSY Netzer: Jewish youth organisation

Salaam Alaikum: Muslim greeting of peace

sauerkraut: fermented raw cabbage

schnitzel: meat fried in breadcrumbs

schtum: silent

seder: the ceremony at Passover

shabbat: Friday night to Saturday night (the sabbath)

Shabbat Shalom: sabbath greeting

Shalom Aleichem: Jewish greeting of peace

Shecoyah: well done

Shema: central Jewish prayer

Shidduch: matchmaker

Shoah: Holocaust

Shofar: ram's horn blown at Jewish New Year

shul: synagogue

siddur: prayerbook

simchas: special occasions

strudel: pastries

succah: booth built at Succot

Succot: Feast of Tabernacles

talit: fringed prayer shawl

teiglach: sticky sweets

tochus: backside

Torah: five books of Moses

tsores: trouble, worries, headaches

tzedakah: charity

yarmulke: same as kippah

Yiddish: language spoken by some Jews

Yom Kippur: Day of Atonement

zaider: grandfather

Acknowledgements

Thank you to Rabbi Dr Michael Hilton, Dr Claire Hilton, Professor David Nicholls, Rabbi Dr Jonathan Romain and Aamina Siddiqi for kindly reading the novel and giving me useful feedback, and to Professor Tony Kushner for his ongoing support.

Any errors, however, are my responsibility and not theirs.

So let me suffer, why don't you?

Praise for *The Water and the Wine*

'Well-turned storylines, excellent character development and a generous portion of the world as lived in the sixties make this a very fine treasure of a book.'

The San Francisco Review of Books

'an enchanting, entertaining read.'

Allan Showalter, *Cohencentric*

'a real tour de force'

Daniel Klein, novelist

'In this very fine novel, Hodes describes the landscape and people with intensity and beauty. Highly recommended.'

Nick Broomfield, film-maker

'a haunting, unforgettable work'

Rebecca Smith, novelist

'Leonard Cohen fans, creatives – and those that love them – and anyone who loves Greece, will enjoy this story.'

Windy City, Chicago

'A delightful novel that brings out the excitement and depth of the creative process... a thought-provoking narrative, an unforgettable work. It's a read that deserves recommendation.'

Book Traveller

'I will be recommending *The Water and the Wine* to the many fans of not only Leonard Cohen but also of romantic novels.'

Anna Maria Tuckett, writer and critic

Printed in Great Britain
by Amazon